BONE
COLD

BONE COLD

DEBRA WEBB

PINK
HOUSE
PRESS

Edited by Marijane Diodati

PINK HOUSE PRESS
WebbWorks
Huntsville, Alabama

First Edition October 2014

ISBN-10: 0692287574
ISBN-13: 9780692287576

Dear Reader,

Writing this story was difficult. Panic attacks are a problem I know too well. Though it has been thirty years, I remember the date and the hour I had my first one. The way a person deals with a challenge like panic attacks or panic disorder is a very personal journey. Please know that Sarah's journey is based on my experience and nothing else. If you suffer from panic attacks, please speak to your physician about the available options that will best help you to face the challenge.

As always, I hope you enjoy the story!

Deb

CHAPTER ONE

"Grab the little bitch!" Jack Coben snarled under his breath, his fingers tightening on the steering wheel. Hell, she was five years old. How fast could she run? His partner's labored puffing as he gave chase echoed in the tiny high tech communications device Coben wore in his ear. He rolled his eyes. The fat bastard sounded like he was the one on the verge of a coronary.

If he couldn't handle something as simple as nabbing a five-year-old kid, he was freakin' useless. Hell, it wasn't like they hadn't done this before. Coben felt his own heart kick with a split second's panic. Failure wasn't an option. His chest tightened abruptly and he cursed himself for forgetting his damned pills.

"Got her," vibrated in the earpiece.

Relief instantly eased the discomfort banding around Coben's heart as efficiently as the digitalis he forgot to stuff into his pocket this morning. "I'll pick you up around the corner," he told his out of shape cohort as he eased off the brake and allowed the van to roll forward. He turned left onto the street that flanked the park then drove slowly until his partner emerged from the woods with the now unconscious kid in his arms.

Coben stomped the brake. The van's side door slid open while the vehicle was still rocking to a stop. "Go!" Nichols sputtered between gasps for breath as he dove into the cargo area.

Three minutes later, they were a safe distance from the area of Chinquapin Park with no sign of a tail. The police scanner mounted under the dash remained gratifyingly silent.

Coben exhaled the final remnants of tension squeezing his chest. By the time the criminally complacent nanny realized the kid was gone, searched frantically for her, and then called the police, Coben and his partner would be long gone.

There would be no witnesses…no clues…nothing.

For all anyone knew the little girl had vanished into thin air. *Poof!* Coben grunted. Who trained these damned nannies?

Rick Nichols squeezed between the seats and plopped into the one on the passenger side. "I'm not taking another chance like that in broad daylight," he warned, swallowed hard, then fought for another breath. "When she turned around and saw me, I thought for sure she was gonna scream."

Thank the pioneers of science for fast-acting drugs, Coben thought wryly. He glanced over his shoulder at the little girl sleeping so peacefully on the stained quilt a few feet behind him. Pretty blond hair adorned with a silky pink bow spilled over the tattered fabric of the quilt. How sweet. He wondered if her *busy* mother had put that bow in herself or if the nanny had done it. For sure, it hadn't been the daddy. The whole freakin' world knew how busy *he* was.

People just didn't know how to appreciate the little things until it was too late. It was definitely too damned late now for this little girl's folks.

Turning his attention back to the man beside him, Coben considered the imbecile's threat for a moment. "You'll do whatever the hell I say, when I say it. Understood?"

Still wheezing as if he'd run a damned marathon, the fat oaf nodded. "Yeah, yeah. I got it." He shifted in his seat to stare at their valuable cargo. "I'm just glad she didn't scream." A beat of silence passed. "What's gonna happen to all these kids?"

Coben barked a laugh. "How the hell do I know? We get paid to bring them in. What happens after that is none of our concern." He slanted Nichols an irritated glance. "Your conscience should've kicked in six kids ago."

Now wasn't the time to grow something he didn't have when this whole thing started. Besides, if Nichols had half a brain he'd know that in cases like this the fewer witnesses left behind the better.

"Yeah, I guess you're right." His partner regarded the kid once more. "Ain't nothing to me as long as I get paid."

CHAPTER TWO

Lieutenant Sarah Cuddahy stared at her reflection in the ladies' room mirror. She looked like hell. The dark circles under her eyes were a dead giveaway that she felt as bad as she looked. No amount of concealer was going to hide the evidence of two weeks' worth of little or no sleep.

"You can do this." Her heart pounded faster and her hands shook, making a liar out of her. "Dammit!" She didn't have time to be in here fighting this battle.

Just do it.

Clutching the bag draped on her shoulder, she surrendered to the inevitable and slipped into a stall. Three whole days she'd managed without the damned pills and here she was back at square one. She was a detective for Christ's sake. She had faced rapists and murderers, and even taken a bullet once. Why couldn't she beat this?

Two months ago, she'd tossed the anti-depressant against her doctor's warning. She'd been cautiously optimistic so far. No lapses back into those deep, dark places that had haunted her for so long. To her credit, she had taken the doctor's advice about distracting herself with activities she'd once enjoyed by spending more time on the treadmill. Somehow, she doubted he'd had that particular activity in mind when he made the suggestion. Yet, it had worked.

Until the first child went missing.

Sarah's hands shook. She had jumped at the opportunity to work the case. On some level, she'd seen it as a test…a way to prove she was the old Sarah again. Then, three more children in the DC area had disappeared. Within the next seven days another two, outside Metro's jurisdiction, had vanished and a Joint Task Force had been formed. Detectives from surrounding jurisdictions were working together with the FBI's support to find the children.

The Task Force commander had chosen her as the lead detective at Metro, in part because no one had more experience with missing children than Lieutenant Sarah Cuddahy. Not only had she worked several cases of child abductions, five years ago her own child had gone missing. Pain and dread knotted in her belly.

The others on the Task Force believed she possessed some vast, intimate knowledge that would somehow prove beneficial to the case. At one time, she had considered herself damned good at tracking down the missing. Her instincts had been razor sharp. Now, the only thing Sarah knew with complete certainty was that she needed to hold it together long enough to get through this investigation.

She pressed her heated forehead to the cool metal of the stall door. Six missing kids were depending on her. The Task Force was gathering for a briefing at this very moment. She was supposed to be in that conference room right now instead of in here…*like this.*

Deep breath, Sarah. Hold it, and then let it go slowly and repeat.

Every second of every minute she hesitated exploded in her head like a weapon discharging.

All she had to do was walk back out there and do her job.

Except the damned panic wouldn't let go. The band around her chest screwed tighter as she tried to draw in those slow, deep breaths. Wasn't happening. If she refused to give in and take a pill, her heart rate and blood pressure would continue to climb. The numbness and lightheadedness would begin, and then the real panic would descend. She knew the routine all too well. To stand here and pretend it wouldn't happen this time was foolish.

Her shrink had told her the panic attacks would go away in time with the proper therapy and medications.

Sarah laughed out loud. "Yeah, right."

She scrubbed a hand over her face. The debilitating episodes were never going away. This was her life now. No matter what she did—throwing herself into work by day and working out until she fell exhausted into bed at night—they always came back when the pressure was on. Four years of on-again-off-again therapy sessions and medication hadn't done a damned thing except keep her disappointed in herself when she failed to avert the next panic attack.

Her shrink would say the problem was with her expectations. *You work too hard, Sarah. Set your standards too high. No one is perfect. This is not a weakness, it's a disorder. Can't you see that, Sarah? The propensity for panic disorder was always there. You suffered a significant trigger, which brought the problem to the surface.*

She didn't care what they called it or how long it had supposedly been there, to her it felt like weakness and she just wanted it to go away.

Hurry! Like a clock spinning out of control, the seconds ticked off in her brain. No use dragging out the inevitable. The others would be waiting for her.

Sarah reached into her bag and fished out the damned prescription bottle and stared at it. In five long years this was the only true relief she had found. She would have a few hours without that insistent sensation of doom and the escalating anxiety. It would bring a blessed reprieve from the shakes, the pounding heart, and the cold, clammy skin. Why resist the one thing she could count on?

Your condition doesn't make you a failure, Sarah.

The shrinks had gotten that part wrong. Sarah had failed as a mother and a wife. All she had left was being a cop. She couldn't risk failing at that, too.

"Enough already." She twisted the cap from the bottle, popped the pill into her mouth, then fumbled with the stall latch to get out. Hands still shaking, she turned on the tap and ducked her head beneath the water. A deep swallow and the first wave of relief was immediate. Not because the pill kicked in that quickly, but because her body knew it was coming.

Swiping her mouth, Sarah stared at her reflection again and hated herself just a little more.

CHAPTER THREE

He was going to kill her this time.

Mary Cashion stood perfectly still while her husband paced the room like a death row inmate anticipating that final walk. He looked ready to blow. His posture…his profile…every muscle had gone rigid with rage. A helpless sinking sensation pulled at her stomach.

Lawrence Cashion had beaten her periodically for the entire fifteen years they had been married. He was always careful that the bruises didn't show. The mental abuse at times defied her ability to articulate the level of ugliness he somehow managed to reach. Her husband could be so very cruel. Mary accepted the words and even the beatings to a degree. It was the only way to survive. She couldn't possibly leave.

Despite all he was behind closed doors, as far as everyone else was concerned he was a respected pillar of the community. He owned his own company and their five-year-old daughter, Cassie, loved him without reservation. Thankfully, he had yet to lay a hand on their child, but Mary couldn't help wondering when that moment would come. How long would it be before he turned that violent temper upon their little girl? It had happened once before…

Anguish rose so sharply inside her that she barely held it in check. If she so much as whimpered right now, she would break the trance he'd slipped into. She had to be strong and pray—pray it would pass. On rare occasions if she held absolutely still, kept all emotion from her face, the frenzy would subside. He'd pace it off, his mind focused inward on images or voices only he could see or hear.

Please, God, let this be one of those times.

Lawrence halted abruptly, his back ramrod straight, his neck flushing above his crisp white collar as if he'd heard her fervent prayer.

Mary held her breath. She resisted the urge to close her eyes against what she knew was coming. She wasn't going to escape this time. Sometimes she wished he would have a heart attack and just die the way his father had. Strange, she realized, despite being the daughter of a minister and having spent a lifetime as a devout Christian, she felt no guilt at the thought.

If only she dared to go to the police. No. That opportunity had passed. There would be no going to the police and Lawrence knew this. Their secret—the vow they had both taken to protect their secret—would not allow that step.

The door burst open.

"Daddy! Daddy! I made a picture for you today!"

Mary's heart stumbled, yet her entire body remained paralyzed with utter terror as she watched their unsuspecting daughter barrel straight up to her father waving her latest artwork.

She'd been napping when Mary came downstairs. *Please, God, don't let him hurt my baby.* The child had never burst in on one of his rages before. Mary didn't know how he would handle the unexpected intrusion.

For five excruciatingly long seconds, he just stood there staring wild-eyed down at their child, his profile chiseled in granite, the color of rage still licking a wide path along his neck and jaw.

"It's Wiggles," Cassie explained, excitement lighting up her pretty brown eyes as she pointed to her finger paint rendering of their small Dachshund.

"Well! Let me see what you've got there," her father said, his voice only slightly strained and booming with pride.

Relief washed away terror's grip and Mary sagged. The breath she'd been holding whooshed out of her lungs as Lawrence knelt down to inspect the primitive drawing.

"See," Cassie was saying, "there's his tail and there's his nose."

As if the threatening tension he'd exuded mere moments ago had never even existed, Lawrence enumerated the various fine details of his daughter's work. He smiled lovingly as Cassie pointed out she'd somehow managed to give Wiggles only three legs.

When he laughed out loud, Mary knew she had escaped.

It was over.

For now.

Standing in his study watching their daughter hug her beloved father, Mary knew the decision she had made was the right one. No matter how many times she had failed before, she had to try again. The business card she had hidden beneath the floor mat in her car and the money she had slipped aside for three years now were all she needed. She could do it with the right help and the police wouldn't have to be involved.

She had to do it.

Cassie was still small enough that her sweetness, her innocence could turn the tide of his rage...just barely. But that wouldn't last forever.

Then it would be too late.

Again.

CHAPTER FOUR

Joe Adams leaned back in his leather executive's chair and looked across the wide expanse of his mahogany desk. He smiled. He had them by the short hairs and they knew it. Nothing was going to stop this bill from passing the Senate. These two were the sole holdouts he needed on his side.

"Come now, gentlemen," he said when the discontented silence dragged on. "It isn't that bad."

"It's blackmail." Senator Bill Fletcher, an Idaho farm boy turned public servant, narrowed his gaze as a glimmer of courage prodded his conscience.

How people did change.

"I believe the term blackmail is a bit strong in this instance," Joe offered. "I like to think of the offer as a compromise."

Senator Bryan O'Neal made a dissatisfied grunting sound. O'Neal hailed from Kansas and, like all Midwesterners he thought he was a cut above the jaded folks on the eastern side of the continent.

Joe smiled again as he thought of how naïve most young senators were when they first got themselves elected to office. Oh, how they were going to change things in Washington. Determined men and women who couldn't wait to get to the Capitol and make their mark. With a little time, reality sank in and the dream crashed like a kite in an electrical storm. By the second term, if they made it that far, all their wide-eyed innocence had vanished. The two men currently seated across from Joe were both past that *virgin* first term. They knew precisely what he was up to and there wasn't a damned thing either of them could do about it. It was the way things worked on Capitol Hill.

"You have a comment you'd like to make, Senator O'Neal?" Joe inquired, feeling smug with the victory coursing through his veins.

"I think we understand each other," O'Neal said flatly.

"Very well." Joe pushed to his feet and offered his hand. "I'll consider it done."

The two dazed senators rose from their seats, each taking a turn to, without conviction, shake Joe's hand. He knew with complete certainty what they wanted to do was climb across his desk and strangle him, but that wouldn't happen. This conversation would never leave the room, yet the ramifications it carried would move a certain bill through the Senate.

Joe had the one thing he needed on both men. And he intended to use that information to the fullest possible extent. For the good of the country, of course.

When the two had exited his office, Joe resumed his seat and scanned the messages his secretary had given him prior to the impromptu visit. The very idea those two would think for a second they could talk him out of his stand was absurd. He wasn't in the habit of backing off or of looking the other way. He needed this bill to move forward without interference for reasons O'Neal and Fletcher, as well as the rest of the country, could never know.

Joe's smile slid back into place. He liked the feeling of power that surged through him each time he considered how close he was to his ultimate goal. A very large debt would finally be settled. The buzz of the intercom snapped him from his pleasant reflections. "Yes, Connie."

"Senator, there's a man on line one for you. He…" She cleared her throat. "He identified himself as a police detective. He says it's an emergency."

Joe let her off the hook with a distracted, "That's fine, Connie." He'd asked her to hold his calls, but this sort of interruption couldn't be helped. He punched the blinking light that would connect him to line one. "Joe Adams."

He never referred to himself as senator. It sounded incredibly pompous. While he couldn't deny a good dose of arrogance in his attitude these days—what politician didn't possess at least a little— Joe still remembered his upbringing. He'd grown up on a farm in a tiny town in Virginia that wasn't even on the map today, much less forty years ago when he'd watched his first presidential address. He'd known what he wanted then and there.

"Senator Adams, this is Detective Aaron Kline from Alexandria PD."

"Yes, detective, how can I help you this afternoon?" As he waited for the detective to continue, Joe leaned back in his chair and considered whether he should take his family out to dinner tonight. He felt like celebrating.

"Sir, I'm afraid I have some difficult news."

The grave sound of the detective's voice yanked Joe back to full attention. "What's happened?" he heard himself ask, as if someone else were speaking. The transformation required only a mere fraction of a second…the tone of the detective's voice more than his words awakened long slumbering demons. Instantly, the vivid image of his wife and daughter flashed in Joe's mind, sending a trickle of apprehension through him.

Not again. The urge to wail those two words very nearly overwhelmed him. He couldn't bear that kind of pain again. Before he could stop it, snippets of memory from six years ago tumbled one over another in his brain, resurrecting a haunting devastation that tore at his heart.

"Sir, I'm sending someone to pick you up and bring you to the precinct. Your wife will be waiting here for you. We'll go over all the details together."

*His wife…*not his wife and his daughter…not his family.

"Dear God, man, just tell me what's happened!" Fear exploded inside him, rupturing the thin veneer of propriety, leaving behind agonizing dread. Blood roared in his ears, the sound echoing the *nooo* trapped in his throat.

"Sir," the detective said solemnly, "your daughter is missing. We don't know yet—"

"I'm on my way."

Joe didn't bother listening to the rest of the detective's grim statement. He wasn't waiting and it didn't matter why or how or what the cops did or didn't know yet.

It only mattered that his daughter was missing.

There must be a mistake. God wouldn't be that cruel. He wouldn't let this kind of tragedy strike twice in one lifetime.

It had to be a terrible mistake.

CHAPTER FIVE

The briefing had ended an hour ago. The members of the Task Force had wandered out of the conference room knowing no more than they had when they'd arrived. Sarah stayed behind, studying the six faces posted on the case board. The children were four and five years of age. All were from homes of privilege and wealth. Yet not a single ransom demand had materialized in any of the cases, not even after hefty rewards were offered.

A scowl worked its way across her forehead. Six innocent children. Six sets of parents ready, willing, and perfectly capable of handing over enormous sums of cash, but no takers.

And no bodies.

Two weeks had elapsed since the first child went missing. If money were the motivation a ransom demand would certainly have been made well before now. The MOs were consistent. Each child had been nabbed during the course of a routine activity on a day that was in no way out of the ordinary—with the exception of the abduction. One moment the little boy or girl was there, the next he or she was gone. *Vanished.*

The parents in each case had been cleared of suspicion. Friends and relatives had been endlessly scrutinized without discovery of a single pertinent detail. Nothing. Not the first indication that the kidnappings were carried out by anyone even remotely connected to the families existed. The families were not linked by school or church or by personal or professional relationships.

Since the victims were both male and female that marginally narrowed down the type of predator. Most child predators preferred one or the other. The ages of the victims appeared to be a part of the selection process. There was no pattern in hair or eye color or other physical attributes. Poor health had not served as an element of elimination since one child had recently developed a rare form of leukemia.

Sarah forced away the whispers of dark memories that attempted to invade her head. *Focus. You have to focus.* She stretched her neck and rubbed at the tension there. Every imaginable possibility that might connect the children had been considered and none had been found. Age and wealth appeared to be the only common factors. Anyone who might have seen or heard anything in recent weeks had been interviewed. Did the parents argue?

Was the child happy? Were there hidden financial woes? The same questions had been asked over and over. Was there a life insurance policy? What was the long-term prognosis in the case of the child suffering from ill health? Had the doctors said anything that may have led the parents to believe the child would be better off dead?

There was no evidence to gather and analyze, except for one apparent slip up. After the fourth victim had been abducted, a male size ten shoeprint had been lifted from the scene. That was it—one shoe print and nothing else.

The person or persons behind the abductions were professionals. The unknown subjects, unsubs as the feds called them, were in and out in a flash. No signs of struggle or force. No fingerprints left behind, not the first hint of DNA, and no witnesses. There was no apparent pattern to the locations selected and no emerging hypothesis as to who might be next.

Bottom line, they were desperate for any kind of evidence.

Sarah heaved a sigh. If they didn't find any evidence the children might never be found.

Like Sophie…

A shudder went through her. As hard as working this investigation was for her on a personal level she refused to give up. She needed to do this. She wanted to find these children alive. Maybe it was a pipe dream, but she was hanging on.

Part of her desperately needed to prove she could still handle this type of investigation with the same relentless determination she did all others. Chief Reginald Larson had almost said no when she asked for the case. He probably would have if he'd known then it would turn into a multi-jurisdiction task force investigation. A lot was riding on her ability to get the job done—for her and, more importantly, for the children.

Won't make up for not finding your own daughter.

Sarah blocked the taunting voice and concentrated on the faces on the timeline. Where were these children being kept? Assuming they were still alive. What was the purpose of the abductions, if not for money?

Every member of the Task Force agreed that the children were either being used for perverse sexual services, or were being sold for other even more terrifying purposes. One of the first motives considered, given the ages, was that the children had been taken for their organs but that didn't make sense in the case of the sick child. Since the child had been snatched from the hospital there was no way the unsub didn't realize the child was ill. Whoever was behind these puzzling abductions had been too meticulous to screw up that badly.

The FBI's official stand on the case, as of this evening's briefing, was that the children were more likely victims of human traffickers. In light of how well planned and rapidly executed the abductions were no one wanted to go with the theory of a single serial predator.

There was no denying the unsub was smart and organized, it was the motive that truly worried Sarah.

She allowed that last realization to echo through her. She'd known his kind before…had prayed she never would again.

You failed that time, Sarah. Why on earth would you believe you could succeed now?

She pushed the thought and the fear aside. The shrink she'd stopped making time for six months ago would warn Sarah that she was venturing into dangerous territory. After all, three months in a posh treatment center and nearly four years of hit-or-miss therapy hadn't fixed her.

You must allow yourself to grieve, Sarah.

She didn't want to grieve. She wanted to work.

Sarah squared her shoulders. "I can do this." She said the words out loud, listened as they resonated in the empty room. All she had to do was keep looking and she would find the thing they were all missing.

No matter that everyone else had called it a day she couldn't go yet. She had to try just a little longer. Maybe something…anything she'd overlooked during all those interviews and hours of studying reports and verifying facts would bob to the surface. Every hour that passed without a break in the case lessened the likelihood the children would be found, alive anyway.

That part was killing her.

"Sarah?"

She turned away from the timeline as Chief Larson entered the conference room. "I won't be here much longer."

Sarah expected him to remind her that working fifteen-hour days wouldn't help anyone, least of all her. One of these days she was going to remind him that he kept the same hours himself. If it wasn't good for her it wasn't good for a man so close to retirement either.

Larson studied the board for a long moment before he finally spoke. "We may have number seven."

Her pulse rate bumped into a faster rhythm. "Where?"

"Alexandria. The locals have started a grid search already. Crime scene unit's been dispatched. The parents are being interviewed right now."

Sarah squeezed her eyes shut for one brief second. *Please let him have made a mistake this time.* "Do you have any other details?"

The chief's broad shoulders slumped a bit. As tall and strong as he was he looked as weary and defeated as Sarah felt. "Age five, female. Snatched from the park practically under her nanny's nose."

Nanny. Another child of a wealthy family. Sarah raked a shaky hand through her hair, wishing she'd worn it up and out of the way today. "I don't suppose he left any evidence behind?"

"Nothing we know about yet."

"Nothing is all we have," she said tightly, her anger stirring. "Except a damned size ten male athletic shoe and we don't even know for certain if it belongs to the unsub."

The chief paused to draw in a mighty breath. "Well, Detective," he said, "I'm afraid this one only gets worse."

Sarah stilled. Larson rarely referred to her as detective and usually only when things were going to hell in a hurry. "How so?" she demanded, her fingers curling into hard balls at her sides in hopes of holding onto the anger. She needed the anger to keep her going.

"The little girl's name is Katie Adams." One eyebrow winged toward his thinning hairline in punctuation. "As in Senator Joseph Adams' one and only child."

Sarah shook her head. "The media's going to have a field day with this one."

They needed the community helping, not panicking. Having a well-known politician's personal life dissected in the news outlets would shift the focus away from the search for missing children.

"There's nothing we can do about that, unfortunately."

"If those kids are still alive and our guy gets scared…" She didn't have to say the rest. Larson understood all too well what would happen then. The unsub would disappear and the children would be lost.

The chief rested his grim gaze on hers. "It's late, I know, but Captain Andrews wants you to go to Alexandria PD and interview the parents tonight."

John Andrews was the Task Force commander. Each detective and agent on the Task Force was assigned to a particular aspect of the investigation. For Sarah, it was the family interviews. She, better than anyone, could empathize with the devastated parents. She'd been there.

What was she thinking? She was *still* there.

You can lie to everyone else, Sarah, but you can't lie to yourself.

"I'll head there now." The hour didn't actually matter. If Sarah went home, the chances she would sleep were negligible at best.

"Tread carefully with this one, Sarah. Keep in mind that Adams is not just a parent, he's a U.S. Senator."

"Got it, Chief."

For a couple of minutes after Larson left Sarah stood there gazing at those sweet, innocent faces. "All we need is one break and we'll find you."

The promise she hoped she could keep echoed in the empty room as she walked out.

CHAPTER SIX

Sarah flashed her ID at the duty officer's desk. "I'm here to see Detective Kline. I believe he's expecting me."

The sergeant checked his notes and nodded. "Yes, ma'am." He pointed down the corridor to the left of his desk. "The elevators are that direction. Third floor. You'll find Kline in the conference room. You can't miss it."

"Thank you."

For a Friday night the place was pretty quiet. She pressed the call button at the bank of elevators. It wouldn't be that way at any of the Districts in D.C. Sarah preferred the hustle and bustle. It kept her mind off the past and the emptiness that waited for her at home. Staying busy was the only therapy she needed, in her opinion.

The elevator doors opened and she stepped inside. Of course, neither her shrink nor her boss saw eye to eye with her on the matter. Her husband hadn't either. They hadn't agreed on much near the end. Maybe that was why he'd left.

Not true, Sarah. You made him leave.

Sarah closed out that line of thinking as the elevator bumped into motion.

The scene in the third floor conference room was one Sarah knew far too well. She'd witnessed that look of absolute horror and disbelief on more faces than she cared to remember. She still saw it in the mirror every morning. A child was missing. No parent wanted to believe it could happen to them.

"Detective Cuddahy." Aaron Kline stood the moment he looked up and saw Sarah in the open doorway. He gestured to the man cradling his wife against his chest at the end of the conference table. "This is Senator Joseph Adams and his wife Laura."

The senator nodded. The wife never looked up.

Kline indicated the chairs lining the table. "Have a seat and we'll update you on what we have."

As Sarah suspected, they'd found nothing. The team would go back out in the morning, but she doubted they would find anything. The nanny had looked away for mere seconds and the child had disappeared. She'd been wearing pink shorts and a polka dot blouse with a pink ribbon in her long blond hair. She had blue eyes like her mother and a vivacious personality like her father. The last part had come from the mother who managed to choke out the words. Pictures and other necessary items to assist in the investigation had been collected from the Adams' home already.

"Senator, ma'am," Sarah said to each in turn. "I know this is hard. It's undoubtedly the hardest thing you will ever have to face, but right now I need you to listen carefully to what I have to say. The only way I can help your daughter is if you help me."

A stiff nod from the senator and a vacant stare from the wife was her response.

Sarah remembered the detective who'd said those same things to her. His voice had been somber, but his eyes had given him away. He'd known when he said the words that Sophie was gone for good. Sarah would never see her daughter again. The ability to interact with her husband would slowly but surely deteriorate. Her life would never be real again. Nothing, except work, would ever matter to her again.

Everything he *hadn't* told her had come to pass.

"The first forty-eight hours after an abduction are the most crucial," Sarah went on, exiling the painful memories to that dark place where they belonged. "My questions will be direct and to the point. I need you to answer each one to the best of your ability." She reached into her bag and retrieved the audio recorder. After placing it on the conference table, she pressed the record button and settled her gaze back on theirs hoping to relay a semblance of calm organization.

"I'm taping this interview so we can listen to it over and over as we search for evidence that will facilitate our investigation in finding your daughter."

The couple stared mutely at her. Sarah imagined both had gone numb at this point. Nothing felt real.

Typical. She needed all the information she could get before that numbness wore off and reality set in again.

"Anything that pertains to your daughter, anything at all, could be useful no matter how seemingly insignificant," she continued. "Is she involved in any sports or hobbies? Dance or music lessons? I need to know every individual she comes into contact with on a regular basis, even those she rarely sees. This abduction may be the result of a single contact. Her pediatrician, her dentist, the person who trims her hair. Friends. Relatives. Don't leave anyone out. At this stage of the investigation, everyone is a suspect, including the two of you."

Mrs. Adams gasped, indignation joining the terror in her red, swollen eyes, but the senator remained stoic, his expression unflinching.

"First," Sarah began, "are there any problems with the two of you, marital, financial, or otherwise?"

Three hours later Sarah had all she was going to get. The Adamses, as well as Detective Kline, looked exhausted. "Just one last question, Senator," she said when they had all risen in preparation for ending the interview.

The annoyed look he pointed in her direction was nothing more than his weariness. She didn't take it personally.

"Are you certain there is no one who has a grudge against you? You've made quite a reputation on Capitol Hill for standing by your beliefs and not being swayed. You've unquestionably made a few enemies along the way."

Something changed in the senator's demeanor. The shift was subtle, but Sarah noticed.

"Detective Kline," he said without taking his eyes off Sarah. "Would you show my wife back to your office while I speak with Detective Cuddahy privately for a moment?"

"Of course, Senator."

Obviously too weak with emotions to argue Mrs. Adams followed Detective Kline without comment.

When the door had closed behind them, the senator stared long and hard at Sarah for a moment longer before he spoke. "If I had any enemies capable of this I would have said so up front. Now." He pulled in a big breath. "Give it to me straight, Detective. What are we looking at here? I've read about the children who've gone missing the past week or so."

Sarah kept her expression carefully schooled. Adams didn't know the half of it if his assessments were based on what he'd read in the papers. Telling him wasn't going to change anything. Not really. Or maybe she just didn't want to go down that road at this time of night. She, too, was exhausted.

She braced for his reaction. "We believe there could be a connection."

"Dear God." The words were scarcely more than a wounded moan.

"We can't be sure of anything yet. Your case may be different. There could be a ransom demand.

There could be evidence that points to an entirely different MO. Forensics may turn up important clues that will lead us to your daughter. All the proper alerts have been issued, the search is ongoing."

Adams shook his head slowly from side to side. "You're holding back on me, Detective. I can see it in your eyes."

Sarah had trained herself long ago never to give away her emotions. He was fishing. "Senator, I wish I could give you more, but it's too early to have any answers."

"So you'll waste precious time interrogating friends and relatives," he said savagely, his anger building with each word as he concluded the worst... the *truth*, "on enemies I don't have. You know more than you're telling me. I demand full disclosure."

"I wish that was true, sir," she responded frankly. "If I were holding out on you that would mean I have some sort of substantial lead...some hope of finding answers." She tossed the idea of beating around the bush. Why hide it? He would know by morning. He would push everyone involved until he was told all there was to tell.

The color drained from his face. "It's worse than I thought," he said, his tone unexpectedly soft... the force barely enough to carry the words across the room. His eyes held a new kind of terror. "How many are missing?"

Sarah moistened her lips and told him what he wanted to hear. "We have six missing children— seven if your daughter's abductor doesn't demand a ransom. If," she cleared her throat of the emotion clogged there, "her body isn't found."

"Seven children," he repeated, a new wave of shock visibly setting in. "And no leads?"

She shook her head. "Not one."

CHAPTER SEVEN

Sarah parked at the curb and stared up at the Victorian townhouse lit only by the meager glow from the street lamp. She wished now she'd left a light on, but she hadn't known she would be home so late though she should have. She couldn't remember the last time she'd made it home before dark.

Summoning the necessary strength she opened her car door and stepped out onto the walk. When she closed the door and activated the locking alarm a dog somewhere up the deserted street barked in protest. Sarah glanced toward the desolate howl and shivered. All the other houses were dark like hers, the residents tucked in for the night.

She wondered if they would sleep so peacefully if they knew what she knew.

Seven missing children.

Sarah trudged up the steps toward her front door, the exhaustion boring deeper. It felt suffocating, overwhelming. Crushing.

"Sarah!"

She whipped around at the sound of the female voice on the street behind her. Her heart bumped hard against her sternum in the three seconds required for her to recognize the voice.

Carla Parsons stood at the bottom of the steps, her face dimly lit by the ancient street lamp. She looked much older than she had the last time Sarah saw her. How long had it been? Eight or nine months? They talked by phone from time to time but not recently. Those dark memories she worked so hard every waking hour to keep at bay, whispered inside her, chilling Sarah to the bone.

"Carla." Sarah waited on the landing separating the twin sets of steps that led from the walk to her front stoop. "Are you all right?" It was two a.m. Had there been a break in her son's case? One Sarah hadn't heard about? Whatever it was, Carla obviously couldn't wait to share it.

"I've been waiting for you to come home."

The waif thin woman climbed another step, careful to keep her gaze steady on Sarah as if she feared she might disappear. As she neared, Sarah noted the new lines on her face. The loss of her son had taken a heavy toll. No one lived through the loss of a child without suffering the visible as well as the invisible costs. Sarah knew that better than anyone.

"Waiting? How long?"

"Since around eight."

Sarah sat down on the landing, too tired to do this standing up. "Carla, why didn't you call my office? I could've warned you that I wouldn't be home until late."

The other woman's shoulders slumped with her own exhaustion as she took a seat next to Sarah. "I didn't want to talk on the phone. I needed to do this in person. Waiting wasn't a bother." She looked at Sarah, hope mingling with the desperation that usually inhabited her sunken eyes. "I'd use just about any excuse not to go home."

Carla's son had been missing for five years, like Sophie. Josh Parsons had been six at the time. Sophie was only five. They'd disappeared a week apart. Since Sarah hadn't been able to work the case she and Carla had taken every possible step behind the scenes to find their children, including joining a support group. The longer their children were missing the more they fell apart. Sarah had taken a leave of absence from work for those first few months. Carla had been fired from her job.

Months and years passed and nothing changed except the other faces in their support group. New parents, fresh from losing a child, would wander into a meeting. Others would give up and stop coming. Sarah and Carla had stayed with the meetings longer than most. Then Carla's husband had died. Eventually Sarah's had decided to move on with his life. Tom, the man she had married seemingly a lifetime ago, had tried to make Sarah see that at some point they had to start living again. She couldn't do it, not without Sophie.

Sarah had promptly slipped over the edge after that. Even she had recognized the downward spiral but she hadn't been able to stop it. The crash and burn wasn't her husband's fault. She'd been on the brink for a while. The trip into that dark abyss had earned Sarah three months in a ritzy place with a fancy name that had been nothing more than a mental hospital. She'd come out no closer to being healed than when she'd gone in. There was no true recovery from the loss of a child. A part of her was broken and it couldn't be fixed.

The very day Sarah had been released Carla had overdosed. In truth, Sarah had been contemplating the same thing. Ironically, Carla was the one reason she hadn't. For two days after the overdose Sarah had sat in that hospital room next to Carla's bed. She'd held the other woman in her arms and begged her not to give up. A promise that Sarah would always be there for her was the only way Carla would swear not to try suicide again. Sarah had been forced to forgo the idea of permanently checking out for Carla's sake.

She pushed away the crushing memories. "Has there been a new development in Josh's case?" That couldn't be right. Sarah would have heard.

Carla averted her gaze once more and Sarah suppressed the urge to sigh. Whatever she'd come to say or to ask Sarah wasn't going to like it. They'd been down this road before…too many times.

"There's this man," Carla began hesitantly. "He's kind of like a private investigator."

Carla had hired three private investigators during the first two years after Josh's disappearance. Sarah and Tom had hired a couple, too. Eventually, Sarah had realized they couldn't help them anymore than the cops or the feds could. She wished for a way to save Carla from further hurt. Sarah could tell her not to get her hopes up too high, but why shatter whatever meager hope she had left.

What about you, Cuddahy? What happened to your hopes? Sarah clenched her jaw and evicted that damned little voice that refused to leave her alone even when she collapsed into her drug-induced sleep. Call her a quitter, call her a bad mother, Sarah had finally reached that numb zone and she couldn't look back anymore. For her, it was the only way to survive.

"He has a good reputation and there's something special about him," Carla went on. "I think this time will be different."

That last part gave Sarah pause. "What do you mean *special?*" Anytime a private dick claimed to have some special skill Sarah always grew suspicious. It usually meant the guy was a con artist.

"He can sense things…pick up vibes of some sort. I've spoken to several people he's helped in the past." Carla looked so desperate for anything at all to hang onto. "I really think he might be able to find Josh and Sophie."

When you couldn't. Carla didn't have to say the words.

For the first three and a half years after Sophie and Josh's abductions, not a night passed that Sarah didn't ask herself what she could have done differently. What Tom and his colleagues at the FBI could have done differently. She had mentally reexamined the evidence and the strategies taken by those investigating the case thousands of times.

Drawing in a deep breath, Sarah readied for a hail of protest. "Carla, you know the chances that he's legit are next to none."

Sarah had visited her share of psychics in the beginning. Desperation made people do things they wouldn't normally do. Tom had even asked a man he'd once worked with in the FBI who supposedly had those *special* senses. A waste of time. Dr. Paul Phillips had been a fraud just like all the rest. Yet, Sarah had clung to any hope. She'd wanted to find her baby so badly she would have given her life to make it happen. Still would. The only difference between then and now is that she didn't dare look much less hope. Sophie was gone.

"I know. I know," Carla admitted. "It's just that he has helped a few." She shrugged. "I have to let him try. I don't care how much it costs. It's worth any risk if there's even a remote chance he can find my boy." She looked to Sarah hopefully. "If he finds Josh, he might find Sophie."

Sarah bowed her head and stared at the cracked mortar between the bricks at her feet. The pain of hearing her daughter's name spoken aloud was still nearly unbearable. There were a lot of things she could say right now, negative things mostly, but no advice she had to offer would change Carla's mind. So why hurt her with the truth? As long as she was looking, she had hope. Maybe that was why Sarah had lost hers.

"I know what you mean," Sarah relented. "If there's any chance this guy can help, you should grab onto the opportunity with both hands."

Carla nodded enthusiastically. "That's what I thought. What do I care how much it costs? When the life insurance money my husband left is gone, it's gone, but until then I have to do whatever I can to find him."

Carla didn't say the rest, but Sarah knew what she was thinking. *I can't be like you.*

"I wish I could…help." Sarah couldn't go there again.

Carla laid a hand on her arm. "I know. It's okay. I'm doing this for both of us."

For a long moment they said nothing. The strong connection they'd shared five years ago still hummed just beneath the wall Sarah had built to block the pain. She and Carla had never met until their children disappeared. Two shattered souls adrift on the same desolate ocean looking for any kind of life raft.

Sarah drummed up a shaky smile. "I tell you what, before you become this guy's client and lay down a retainer, let me check him out. If he's clean, then I say go for it."

Carla looked away. "I've checked his references."

Sarah placed a hand over hers. "I know you have and you're probably right in deciding to hire him, but give me a couple of days to dig a little deeper. It couldn't hurt."

After a beat or two of indecision Carla finally dredged up a faint smile. "All right. Like you said, it couldn't hurt. Just let me know as soon as you can. I'd like to get the ball rolling."

"Forty-eight hours is all I need," Sarah promised. "I'll give you something then."

After an awkward farewell hug, Sarah watched as Carla climbed into her car and drove away. The smile Sarah had tacked into place wilted the instant her taillights were out of sight.

Five long years Carla had focused solely on the search for her son. Each individual had to cope in their own way…had to come to terms with the reality in their own time. Some took longer than others. And some, like Sarah, just skipped over certain phases with work and pharmaceuticals.

She unlocked her front door, entered the code for the security system so it would stop beeping a warning and kicked off her shoes. The cool hardwood felt like heaven beneath her tired feet. She hung her keys on a hook on the coatrack right next to the dog leash. She'd had a dog once. Tom had brought him home six months before Sophie was born. A big, black Lab pup they'd named Sam. Sam had disappeared the same day as Sophie. She and Tom had decided that Sam had gone after Sophie and gotten lost. Sarah still looked twice whenever she passed a big old black lab.

She stalled, closed her eyes for a moment to clear her mind of the memories.

No looking back.

What she needed was a little help with shoring up her wobbly defenses. She wandered to the CD player and sorted through the stack of loose CDs until she found the one she wanted. As the lazy notes drifted through the air, she snagged a long neck bottle of beer from the fridge and plodded up the stairs to her bedroom. She allowed a long slug of the cold brew to slide down her throat, and then she held the bottle to her forehead with one hand as she struggled out of her slacks with the other.

Do not mix with alcohol. The warning on her prescription label filtered through her mind. She dismissed it. What was the worst it could do? Kill her?

Sarah laughed. "Can't kill someone who's already dead."

Leaving a trail of clothing behind her, she made her way to the shower, adjusted the spray and temperature of the water, then climbed in and leaned against the cool tile wall. Content to feel the steam rising around her, she took her time and finished her beer. Eventually, she redirected the spray and allowed the hot water to sluice down her body. She moaned softly as the heat instantly started to relax her tired, aching muscles.

Too spent to shut the memories off, images of Tom filtered through her mind. Deep down where she didn't allow anyone else to see, she missed her husband. The trouble with that was, even if he still wanted her, she couldn't be with him anymore. She couldn't live that lie. Disgust welled in her throat. He knew the *truth*. She heard it in his voice, saw it in his eyes. He never mentioned it, but he knew.

If she'd left work on time that day, she would have been home to take Sophie and Sam to the new dog park that had opened a few blocks from the house. Sarah had promised her daughter, but a big murder case had made her forget. Harriett, the sitter Sophie had loved like a grandmother, had agreed to take them. With Sarah's blessing and infinite relief that she could remain focused on her case, Harriet had leashed Sam and off she and Sophie had gone. No big deal. They had walked to the other parks in the neighborhood on numerous occasions.

Only this time they never made it to the park. Sophie and Sam vanished and Harriett was left dying on the sidewalk. No one saw a single thing until a jogger discovered Harriett's cold body.

Sarah squeezed her eyes shut and forced away the images. She had to keep it together. She had six—make that seven—children counting on her. Each face flashed before her eyes like a movie trailer on a slow forward search.

Sarah heard her cell ringing, but she ignored it. Setting her empty beer bottle aside, she stuck her head under the water to drown out the sound. She didn't want to talk to anyone. She just wanted to relax and to find that black emptiness for an hour or two before the dreams invaded.

Later, dried and clad in a fluffy white terry-cloth robe, she went for another beer. Only one more. Heading back to the stairs she paused as she passed the hall table. She ordered herself to disregard her cell sitting there, likely harboring a new voicemail.

Just go to bed and leave it until morning.

Except she couldn't. With a dry laugh, she listened to the message. Chief Larson's deep baritone rumbled in her ear, relegating the subtle tones of the music to the background. "Sarah, call me." A heavy pause. "I don't care what time it is. This can't wait until you come into the office."

Couldn't be good news. Since she would already have been notified if forensics had found anything on Katie Adams before calling it quits at dark this could only be trouble. Either another child had gone missing or a body had turned up somewhere.

Pulse thumping, she chugged down the rest of the beer, steeled herself for the worst, and punched the chief's contact number. He answered on the second ring.

"It's me. What's up?"

He exhaled noisily…hesitated.

Sarah wished she'd taken her pill already. "Do we have a body?" She didn't want any of the children to be dead. Dammit, she didn't want that. No matter how much evidence they might glean as a result.

"No body."

She wanted to feel relieved, but the resigned undertone in his voice warned her that the news was still bad.

"I'm guessing the Senator has done a little cage rattling. I received a call from Quantico."

The FBI was part of the Task Force. Maybe they were sending another profiler from the Behavioral Analysis Unit. Sarah didn't have a problem with more insight. "I don't see the big deal." She said the words a little crankier than she'd intended, but she was overtired and more than a little punchy.

"It's Tom, Sarah. Your husband is coming and he wants to talk to *you*."

For something like ten seconds Sarah felt too stunned to speak. Tom's was the last name she'd expected to hear. *What the hell?* "Why is he coming? Isn't that a conflict of interest or something?"

"I asked the same question," Larson assured her. "He believes these missing kids are related to an ongoing case he's investigating. I got the impression it's a high priority case with a major classified stamp on it."

Sarah shook off the disbelief. "When will he be here?" There went any chance of sleep tonight— this morning actually. The final hours before dawn would be spent trying to strategize ways to deal with an up-close encounter with Tom.

"Noon," Larson said. "He asked for a briefing at one."

Sarah sat her newly emptied bottle aside and raked her fingers through her damp hair. "I don't like this," she muttered, more to herself than to her boss. She plopped down on the stairs and braced her head in her hand. She wasn't ready to see him again. Tom would be watching her every step…analyzing her.

"I don't like it either. Listen, Sarah, the truth is, I was worried about you being a part of this investigation, particularly once things started to escalate, but I've been watching you. You've still got it, Sarah. Those kids need you."

It had taken nearly a year after leaving the treatment center for her to get comfortable in her own skin again. She had her moments, like today when the panic had gotten the better of her, but she managed and she was growing stronger every day. She inhaled a deep, bracing breath. If finding these kids meant facing Tom she would have to find a way to do it.

"I'm not backing off." She had been on this case since the beginning. She wasn't going anywhere until it was done. "I'm in until the end."

"That's what I wanted to hear. See you in a few hours." The chief ended the call with a final order for her to get some sleep.

Sarah seriously doubted that was going to happen.

CHAPTER EIGHT

Lawrence Cashion woke with a raging headache. He straightened, pain streaking through his muscles as the reality of where he was penetrated the lingering haze of a hangover. Wiggles licked his hand and he cursed and shoved the annoying animal away. Whimpering, she scrambled for the closest piece of furniture to cower under.

Muttering a string of hot expletives, all self-related, he swiped his hand on his trousers and then scrubbed it over his jaw. He swore again when he encountered stubble and drool, neither of which fit with the image he had worked hard for more than a decade to build. He'd fallen asleep in his chair.

"Fool," he growled, disgusted with himself for giving in to the temptation of alcohol after more than five years of sobriety. He clenched his jaw against the continued protest of his muscles as he pushed out of the wing chair.

A glass and an empty bourbon bottle lay on the sand colored carpet next to the chair he'd vacated. Whatever contents he hadn't managed to consume during the night's binge had absorbed into the expensive wool fibers, yellowing them.

He cursed himself some more and staggered from the room. He stared listlessly at the stairs for a moment before tackling that climb. What he needed was a shower and a steaming pot of coffee. He started up the stairs, one slow step at a time. Thank God it was Saturday and he didn't have to worry about going into the office. He didn't need a mirror to know his eyes would be bloodshot, and his face would be flushed with the signs of his lost struggle with the bottle. He'd seen that image too many times in the past. He'd hoped he wouldn't see that face again.

What was done was done. He shuffled through his bedroom and into the en suite bath. Nobody was perfect. It wasn't as if he was the first man who'd fallen off the wagon. He had always enjoyed a good drink, there was no denying that fact. Had it not been for the blackouts he'd suffered he probably would never have given up the booze he loved so dearly.

He sighed and flipped on the bathroom light. He figured he'd inherited the trait from his old man. As he peeled off his shirt, the memories from his childhood clicked one after the other through his mind like a bad fairytale. In each and every one the overriding theme was the same—his father on or after a bender, with no memory of what he'd done or where he'd been.

His loving, however undisciplined, father had eventually given up the bottle for that same reason. The change had made him even harder to live with. After years of taking his misery out on his family he'd died a bitter, unhappy man. Well, Lawrence had no intention of allowing that to happen to him. He had the situation under control. So what if he'd slipped up last night? It was the first infraction in years. Besides, he'd been entitled. That cocky bastard Rupert Wendell had won the government contract Lawrence had worked his ass off for. He'd deserved that contract. It would have put him back on easy street. Everyone knew the contract should have been his. Now he had to deal with the questioning looks and the murmuring behind his back.

He hated that feeling. Made him feel the way he had as a kid back in school. Everyone had known his old man was a drunk.

Lawrence kicked aside his shoes and then his trousers. As if that hadn't been enough to kill his day, he'd come home and dinner hadn't even been ready.

It was *her* that had tipped him over the edge.

He gritted his teeth as he considered all that he'd done for his wife. All she had to do was take care of the house and their daughter. That's all. She couldn't even handle those measly tasks. She knew better than to set him off.

Tamping down his fury before it got the better of him, Lawrence reached into the shower stall and flipped on the spray of water. He shivered as the first cold droplets splashed his arms. He'd feel better after a good hot shower. Then he'd savor coffee and have a talk with his lovely, however inept, wife.

He frowned as he considered that she apparently wasn't up yet. She usually made sure the coffee was brewed before he arose. He woke to the rich smell of his favorite blend. That was the way he liked it and she knew it. Another little something they needed to discuss.

He rubbed at the ache in his temples, thinking maybe he'd better pop a couple of aspirin now instead of waiting until coffee. Something in his peripheral vision snagged his attention and his fingers stilled in their work. He blinked as he lowered his hand and peered into his open palm.

Red streaked the pale skin of his palm and fingers. Rubbing his thumb and fingers together, he watched curiously as the water from the shower that had splattered on him and the streaks blended, becoming liquid and sticky. What on earth?

He turned his other hand palm up and stared at it. The same reddish tinges marred the skin there, too. As if watching himself from above he lifted his hands to his face and sniffed hesitantly. The distinct metallic odor slammed into him with such force that he stumbled backward, banged into the open shower door.

What the…?

He peered down at himself, noting no injuries.

Fear held him in its choking grip for the space of two frantic heartbeats, and then he barreled into the bedroom. Nearly hysterical with the thoughts whirling in his head, he scanned the meticulously made bed. It hadn't been slept in. The jacket he'd removed and slung across the footboard when he'd come home last evening still lay exactly where he'd left it.

No longer caring about the ache in his skull or the fact that he only wore his boxers, he rushed to Cassie's room. Not a thing looked out of place. Her bed had not been slept in either.

His heart stalled in his chest and he stared down at his bloodstained hands.

What had he done?

CHAPTER NINE

Sarah surveyed the neatly arranged files on the conference table. She had compiled a detailed file on each missing child, including Katie Adams, for today's briefing. She stopped to look up at the new photograph added to the board of doom. The Adams child was such a pretty little girl. Sarah let go a weary breath, her chest aching with the weight of it. Her big smile reminded Sarah of Sophie. Sarah rarely allowed thoughts of her daughter. It was the sole way to maintain her sanity. Today she couldn't seem to get a handle on those forbidden detours into the past.

Tom would be here soon. When he arrived everything she and the Task Force had on the investigation would be ready for his perusal. Getting straight down to business to expedite this meeting was essential for numerous reasons, her mental well-being included. She hadn't seen him in more than a year. However much she told herself she was prepared for the meeting, she really wasn't so sure. The one certainty she understood was that she could not allow this briefing to turn into a rehashing of their family issues.

Your family doesn't exist anymore.

Sarah banished the tender thought. She had to concentrate. So far, they had determined only a few similarities that tied the children together: age, the family's financial status, and the manner of abduction. One of the children had siblings, the rest were onlys. Yet that one victim broke the pattern, eliminating to a significant degree that distinguishing factor.

Sarah rubbed at the throb starting in her left temple. Between Carla's visit and the chief's call about Tom, she'd hardly slept at all. The notion that she might not be able to help these children anymore than she had Sophie and Josh had replayed over and over in her mind during the wee hours before dawn.

Hearing that Tom was coming had started to chink away at her confidence. He knew her far too well. He would see through her carefully constructed façade to all the shattered pieces. Panic trickled through her.

"Sarah?"

She looked up, startled from her troubling thoughts to find Larson looming in the conference room doorway. She steadied herself and mustered a smile. "I'm almost ready."

"There's been another abduction."

Her heart thumped hard once then lodged in her throat. "This morning?" Jesus, whatever his ultimate goal, his timing had bumped up again.

"Last night. We think," Larson amended.

"You think?"

He nodded, stepped into the room, and then closed the door behind him. "Lawrence Cashion, a Silver Springs businessman, reported his wife and daughter missing about ten this morning. He claims they went to a neighbor's birthday party at around six last evening and never came home. The wife's car was found abandoned five blocks from their home near a wooded park."

Sarah digested the information. "What about the wife?"

"That's the twist," Larson continued. "She appears to have been taken as well."

Sarah felt her head moving from side to side before she'd consciously disagreed with this new development. "It doesn't fit our unsub's MO. He only takes children."

Her boss smoothed a hand over his neatly trimmed hair. "This could be totally unrelated, but since the child's age and the family tax bracket fit, we're going to assume this one is ours for now. Captain Andrews wants you to interview Cashion and make a call on whether this one's in or out."

She nodded. "What do we have so far?"

He thrust a report at her. "This was just faxed over. I can try and postpone the briefing with Tom. He's likely on his way already."

"Speaking of Tom," Sarah decided to ask the question that had helped keep her awake most of the night, "why is he meeting with me—with us? Why not Andrews or even one of the agents on the Task Force?" She'd been avoiding his calls for months. Was he using this investigation as an excuse to check up on her?

"I asked that question myself," Larson admitted. "Tom said he trusted your insights. He wants to talk to *you*."

If he thought she was going to change her mind about the divorce, he could think again.

Sarah scanned the details of the Cashion report. Cassandra Cashion, age four, only child, financially secure family. A frown annoyed Sarah's brow. Why would the mother have stopped on the street at night? The car was left on the side of the road in an area where there were no houses, yet only blocks from her home. No indication of car trouble. No flat tire or empty gas tank. Why stop unless to help or to pick up someone she knew? Why hadn't Cashion spotted the car? Surely, he'd gone looking for them before this morning.

"Is someone checking out the husband's alibi?" That part didn't sit right with her. "He could be hoping to blame whatever he's done on our guy."

"A couple of Silver Springs detectives have grilled him unmercifully. He hasn't copped to anything yet, but that doesn't mean he isn't guilty. He claims he was at home all night, but no one can confirm his whereabouts."

The whole story sounded suspect. It would take time to reconstruct the last twenty-four hours in the Cashion family's lives.

The door opened and before he spoke or she looked up Sarah knew Tom Cuddahy had entered the conference room. A shiver swept across her flesh as if the very air had abruptly been charged by his presence.

"Chief Larson, Sarah," he acknowledged, "they said I'd find you here. I'm a little early, I hope that works."

From the corner of her eye, she saw the chief wheel around and thrust out his hand. "Of course. Of course," Larson said, a smile in his voice. "It's been a while."

"Too long," Tom agreed.

Sarah took a deep breath, squared her shoulders, and did what she had to do. "Hello, Tom. I'm sure you'd like to get started, so if you and the chief will take a seat we'll get to it."

Tom walked straight to where she felt nailed to the floor and smiled down at her. Sarah stiffened, terrified he would hug her. If he touched her…

As if he understood that touching was off limits, he gave her a nod. "It's good to see you, Sarah." He searched her face a little longer than was comfortable. "You look well."

She had taken care to dress in a reserved, professional manner today. The navy jacket and slacks along with a conservative white blouse and practical black leather flats completed the all-business image she'd been going for. She'd tucked her dark hair into a thick silver clasp and had kept her hand light when it came to make-up, as she usually did. She wanted him to see a confident woman, a hardworking detective. Not the shattered being he'd carried into that treatment center eighteen months ago.

"I am well. Thank you."

"Good," Tom said, a glimmer of approval in those assessing green eyes.

Sarah could scarcely bear to look. Sophie had his eyes…and his black hair. The memory twisted in her chest.

"How about coffee all around?" the chief said, splintering the tension that had started building the moment her husband entered the room.

"Coffee would be great," Tom announced. "I'm anxious to have a look at what your Task Force has on this cluster of abductions." He indicated the case board.

"No coffee for me." She didn't need the caffeine. "Water, please."

When the chief had disappeared down the long corridor running parallel to the conference room, her attention moved reluctantly back to Tom.

"You really do look good, Sarah," he repeated. "I'm glad."

"I guess you had your doubts about whether I'd ever be all right again." She picked up the main case file she'd compiled and offered it to the man with whom she'd once shared every part of her being. Voices and images flashed in her mind. Her screaming and sobbing. Him pleading with her to listen to reason.

"Sarah, I—"

She held up a hand. "You're here to talk about the missing children."

He gave her a nod and accepted the folder. "Two plus weeks and no clues, no bodies?"

"Nothing. The only conclusion I've reached is that he's collecting them for—" she shrugged, hating like hell that the gesture looked so helpless "—God only knows what."

Tom reviewed the faces on the board. Four little girls and three boys. And maybe another little girl in Silver Springs.

All waiting to be found.

"Well," he turned back to Sarah, "I'm afraid this is far more complicated than just some unsub amassing assets."

Renewed tension slid through her. "You have reason to believe these abductions are connected to something bigger?"

"Let's sit down." The worry in his eyes tugged at feelings she had thought long dead. "There's a lot I need to tell you, Sarah."

CHAPTER TEN

6035 Blair Road, Washington, D.C., 1:15 P.M.

"Where did the blood come from?" he demanded with a grimace. Coben knew better than to harm any of the children. There was blood all over her clothes.

"I had nothing to do with that." Coben shrugged with indifference. "I started watching her late yesterday afternoon. When I saw her out walking alone just before dark I picked her up. Her clothes were already that way."

He wasn't sure he believed Coben, but then, what did he expect. The sort of individual one hired for work of this nature would be less than trustworthy. He'd known that going in and had been willing to take the risk. Procuring the children himself was out of the question. Working from this warehouse was beneath him, but extraordinary steps had to be taken for the moment.

He inspected the child's body thoroughly for injury. "Coben, you know if I discover that you've touched one…"

Coben glared at him, menace glinting in his cold eyes. "Are you accusing me of something?"

His tone was more than a little unsettling. "I'm only saying—"

"Doc, I know what you're freakin' saying. Save it. I just pick the kids up. I have no interest in them or in you. I'm in this for the money, plain and simple." He cocked his head and cast a challenging glower. "Now, are you going to give me the next list of names, or not? I have other things to do."

"Of course." He left the child lying unconscious on the table and crossed the room to his desk. Coben followed close behind him. He handed Coben the file he'd already prepared. "There are two more. I'll need them as quickly as possible. I'm relocating so there is a change in the drop off location. I'll take this one with me, and you'll be properly compensated for the inconvenience of bringing the other two."

Coben accepted the folder and glanced at the new instructions. "I'll bring them together. I'm not driving that far twice.

"As long as I don't see any more of this." He gestured to the bloody garment the child wore. "Whatever happened, I expect you to handle the children with care."

Coben's gaze turned dead calm. "Trust me, Doc. We had nothing to do with that. I don't do nothing I don't get paid for."

He didn't like this one, liked his partner even less. Be that as it may, so far, Coben had performed the gathering quite efficiently.

His gaze shifted back to the newest delivery and his tension eased a bit.

The necessary housekeeping was almost completed.

And then it would be over.

CHAPTER ELEVEN

Tom hadn't been completely honest with Sarah. She looked pale and too thin—almost as thin as she'd been when he'd carried her to the center. His gut clenched at the idea that he had allowed better than a year to pass without seeing her. He'd kept up with her through a source at Metro. From all reports, she was back to the old Sarah as far as work went. Seeing her told him a different story.

No matter how she lied to herself and to those around her, she still had not come to terms with the loss of their child. At first, like him, she had been determined to find their little girl. Eventually, she'd stopped looking and had closed out everyone in her life who wasn't part of her work, including him. Losing their little girl had devastated them both, but in time he had accepted that unspeakable fate and grieved the loss. Sarah refused to grieve. She carried the burden of so much guilt and it was more than she could bear. He would give anything if he could make her see how wrong she was.

"You said we have a lot to talk about. I'm listening." She toyed with the bottle of water her chief had delivered along with Tom's coffee.

He wished there was something he could say to move past this wall she had built between them. Maybe if they had some time alone together he could make some headway. Tom doubted Larson would appreciate a request to let them be for a while. Would anything he did matter in the long run? Sarah was finished with the life they had once shared. If she still felt anything at all for him she hid it well.

Could she see his feelings? What would she think if she learned the truth?

Not important. Not anymore.

Tom cleared his head and moved on. "I've spent the past fifteen months investigating a case involving medical experiments and murder going back several decades. An entire small Tennessee town was caught up in the insane efforts of one scientist." Tom shook his head. "To tell you the truth, it was like something you'd expect to read in a Dean Koontz novel. Certainly not the sort of thing you'd hear about in real life."

"You believe this is somehow related to the abductions we're investigating?" Larson asked.

Before Tom could respond to the chief's question, Sarah protested, "I don't recall seeing anything about a case like that on the news. If it was as shocking as all that why wasn't anyone reporting on it?"

She had no intention of making any of this easy on him. "I do believe they're related," he said in answer to Larson's question before turning to Sarah. "You remember Paul Phillips?"

The widening of her eyes told him she did. "He helped with…yes, I do."

Even now, five years later, she didn't want to say their daughter's name out loud. "Paul was drawn into the case in Tennessee. Almost got himself killed."

"Is he all right?" Concern clouded her dark eyes.

God, how he had missed those beautiful brown eyes of hers His entire being ached just seeing her and knowing he couldn't even touch her.

"He is now, yes." By the time Tom had received word on Paul's location and condition, his friend was lucky to be alive. "It took months for us to get a handle on exactly what had happened. We learned that three brothers had escaped post World War II Germany and settled in this country. Unfortunately, they weren't good guys. They had conducted horrific medical experiments in the Nazi concentration camps."

Sarah's guard dropped ever so slightly with the shock that claimed her face. "That's incredible."

"I still find the story unfathomable." Even the condensed version he dared to share. "We stopped the work the first two brothers had started, but the third was nowhere to be found. Our search led us to a facility in this area we believe he may be using, but we've had no proof until now."

"Can you be more specific about the medical experiments?" Larson prodded.

"Gene manipulation. Illegal methods of conception. The list goes on and on." That was technically more than he should tell anyone, but he needed Sarah to trust him on this.

"There's no mystery," Sarah gestured to the case board, "related to how these missing children came to be with their parents. They have no medical issues in common and none are patients of the same doctor or dentist. I looked for all common denominators. The only ones are age and financial status."

"There is one or two more you may have missed."

Indignation colored her cheeks. "I don't think so."

"They each have a deceased sibling." Tom saw the surprise in her eyes when she realized he was correct. "Each sibling died less than one year before these children were born."

"What's your point?" She turned her hands up. "The children, the missing ones as well as the deceased siblings, were born naturally to their parents. No adoptions. No fertility clinics."

"One of your missing recently developed a very rare form of leukemia. Two others have recently exhibited issues with behavior at school, and the remaining two have suffered a list of minor complications since birth." That was about as vague as he could be and still get his point across.

"None of those issues were mentioned by the parents when I interviewed them. Frankly, I don't see how they tie into your case. Or mine, for that matter." Sarah crossed her arms over her chest, standing her ground.

She wouldn't buy this without more details and Tom couldn't give those to her. "The gene tampering we found in Tennessee comes with side effects called random errors. Sometimes small, other times life-threatening issues that can develop immediately or over time. There's no pattern to how they happen. They come out of nowhere and are completely *random*. We've been watching for abductions or other criminal activities," he motioned to the stack of files, "involving children who have displayed these random errors. So far, these are the first we've identified."

"You're suggesting these parents are holding back important information that could potentially help us find their children?" If her tone wasn't enough to warn him that she thought he'd lost his mind, the dubious expression on her face got the point across.

"If we're dealing with a situation similar to the one we found in Tennessee, the parents are afraid to tell their secret. And even if they do talk, what they're privy to may not be anything that will help us find their children. I doubt the families know about each other so the pattern of abductions wouldn't have set off any alarm bells."

She searched his face and his eyes. His pulse reacted as if she'd touched him. "You're serious."

It wasn't a question. "I am. These children fit the profile. Their families have the means. All we need is just one of them to talk."

A frown furrowed its way across Sarah's brow. "I'm wondering where the motive is. I've interviewed these families. They're socially and financially prominent. None have mentioned having had issues with conception. Where's the motive for getting involved with something like this?"

"That's one of the answers we need to find."

"Let's say for a moment that your theory is correct," Sarah challenged, "why would the unsub want to kidnap these children and miss out on a potential ransom? What's the goal if not money?"

"The dismantling of the research center and clinics related to what went on in Tennessee has given the remaining brother a heads up that we're on his trail. The random errors showing up in these children will lead us to him. He can't let that happen."

"You're right." Sarah put her hands up in surrender. "This sounds like pure science fiction."

"I'm having trouble with your suggestion," Chief Larson spoke up, "that our victims are some sort of genetic designer children? Like clones or something?"

"I didn't say that, Chief," Tom argued.

He didn't want terms like *clone* to end up on the table. He'd already said too much. In fact, he wasn't supposed to be here at all. If he could keep this among the three of them he might just manage to obtain what he needed without the Bureau finding out. To do that, he needed Sarah on his side. More importantly, he needed her trust. It was a big gamble, but it was the only hand he had left to play.

"Then, what are you saying, Tom?"

Hearing Sarah say his name had his pulse reacting again. "I'm saying these children may be a part of dangerous medical research. If that's the case, the children are evidence and we need to find them before that evidence is destroyed."

Sarah didn't like the sound of this. The whole theory was surreal. "Now you're suggesting that the scientist or scientists who did this alleged shady medical research may be snatching the kids to destroy any evidence of what they've done?" It didn't sound any more plausible when she said it than it had when he did.

"That's exactly what I'm telling you."

"Are you working with Scully and Mulder on the X-Files now?" She shook her head. No way was she buying into this. The scenario was too farfetched. And everyone thought she'd gone around the bend that one time.

To his credit, Tom seemed to take her remarks in stride. "Chief Larson, I'd like a few minutes with Sarah, if that's all right."

Larson looked to Sarah. She shrugged. "For the record," her boss rose from the table, "I'm with Sarah on this one. I'll be in my office." He hesitated at the door. "If you need me, Sarah, just say the word."

As the chief left, Tom shook his head. "You know," he raised his hands as if in surrender, "I understand that you're no longer my wife beyond that piece of paper we signed fourteen years ago. I even get that there's a huge canyon of hurt between us, but what I will never comprehend is your refusal to be friends. What did I do, Sarah, to deserve being cut completely out of your life?"

Her heart was pounding before the last word was out of his mouth. How dare he demand an explanation from her period, much less at a time like this! He was fully aware of what he had done. "Unless what you have to say relates to this case, we're through talking." She would not let this turn into an analysis of their shared history. There had to be another agent who could have come with this incredible story.

He dropped his hands. "Fine. You made your point." He tapped the stack of files she'd prepared for him. "I need your help with this, Sarah." When she would have launched an argument, he added, "You've already interviewed the families. I respect the relationships you've forged. We can work together toward the same end. I want to find these children the same as you do."

Sarah laughed. "I see. You want to use the connection I've made with these families to your advantage. Why didn't you start with Senator Adams? Since he called you, surely you can apply a little pressure and get this truth you believe he's hiding."

If she sounded angry and annoyed that was just too bad. She was angry and annoyed. She had seven, possibly eight, missing children. She didn't have time to waste on the FBI's outlandish theories.

"Don't make this harder than it needs to be, Sarah." The concern in his eyes was undeniably genuine. "We have a painful past. If there were any way around the two of us working together that would be the better solution. The fact is we're the ones sitting here. For the sake of those children we need to put the past aside and get the job done."

Her first instinct was to throw something at him. But, he was right so she opted to hold onto the chair arms to keep her hands busy. "Where would you like to start, Agent Cuddahy?" The sooner they got through this the sooner he would leave. "Shall we start with the family of the first victim?"

"Line up as many interviews as possible," he agreed. "I'll review your assessments and get up to speed on where we are."

"No problem." Sarah pushed out of her chair and almost escaped the room before he manacled her arm. His touch sent a jolt surging through her. His fingers burned her skin and her traitorous heart lurched with confusing signals.

"It doesn't have to be this way, Sarah. We can pretend the life we shared never happened if that's what you want, but would it be such a bad thing for us to be friends?"

"Maybe if you'd stop ignoring my petition for divorce we could talk about being friends." She had been pushing for a divorce for better than a year. He kept coming up with reasons not to sign the papers. If he thought dragging his feet would parlay into a friendship he was wrong. He'd had her committed against her will. Did he really believe after a move like that she would ever trust him again? Impossible. She tried to pull free of his grasp. "Sign the papers and we'll discuss the option."

He held on tighter. "Is a divorce really what you want? Are you that certain we're over?"

For two seconds she couldn't answer. Seeing him after all this time confused her, muddled her thinking. She bullied past the uncertainty. "A divorce is the only thing I want from you, Tom. That's all I will ever want."

CHAPTER TWELVE

503 Ivy Circle, Alexandria, Virginia, 6:50 p.m.

The Adams' home was every bit as extravagant as Sarah had expected. Eight thousand square feet or so, the stately home sat on more than half an acre in a prestigious neighborhood only minutes from the park where their daughter had been abducted.

Sarah knew from personal experience all the luxury in the world wouldn't assuage the agony of having a child in jeopardy.

"Why don't we stop beating around the bush here," the senator suggested, "what is it you're asking?"

So far they had interviewed three of the eight missing children's parents. Each couple had gotten nervous when asked about the child who'd died. All had either fallen apart, stopping the interview, or shutdown, effectively doing the same, at this point. Adams was their last chance today. Sarah was reasonably sure if she kept picking at the issue with the other parents she would get the story—if there was one—but she despised the idea of putting these people through any unnecessary discomfort. If Tom was wrong…

Stay on task, Sarah. Don't over analyze.

"You lost your older daughter five years ago," Tom ventured. "Katie was born ten months later, but you chose a different hospital for her birth. In fact, you used a private facility in Maryland."

Sarah kept her mouth shut, though it wasn't easy. This was one of the many things Tom had kept from her. He hadn't said a word about all the missing children having been born in the same private hospital until they interviewed the Myerses. The shouting match in the car after the interview had garnered her the same old tired response, *I can only provide information on a need to know basis.*

Leave it to the feds to keep local law enforcement in the dark. Her lips tightened at the idea. Whatever the hell was going on, they needed answers if there was any hope of finding these children.

Adams frowned, but not before Sarah saw the lockdown on his defenses. That exhausted, worried sick, I-want-to-help expression vanished.

"Did you really just ask about our choice in health care, Agent Cuddahy?"

"I can assure you," Tom began, "investigating this avenue is in the best interest of finding your daughter. We believe there may be a tie-in related to the hospital."

Then came the shock. Sarah had noted the same with the other parents. "Actually, Senator," Sarah interjected, "we're looking at the employees. This may be a disgruntled employee trying to get back at the hospital by abducting high profile patients."

To his credit Tom didn't say a word or stare at her as if she'd lost her mind. She had an advantage over him. She had already interviewed the senator. Secret or no, if he knew something that would help he would react. Perhaps not by answering their questions, but he would make a call or take action of some sort. Though all the parents were wealthy, Adams was the only one with powerful political connections.

"Are you saying all seven of the missing children were born at the Avalon Center?"

"Yes, sir," Sarah answered before Tom could. "All within the same twenty-four month period and all to families of means. There's potentially eight now." Sarah had confirmed that the Cashion child had been born at Avalon as well. She hadn't been able to interview the father yet. He'd had a heart attack. If he was stable enough later this evening she would be able to question him then.

Adams shook his head. "Avalon is a cutting edge facility. They employ only the very best. I checked them out before we made the decision to go there."

"You weren't happy with the hospital where your first child was born?" Tom checked his notes. "She had her tonsils removed there two years before the accident."

"And she died there," Adams said, his voice cold and empty.

"Are you implying malpractice?" Tom pressed. "You never filed a suit."

"She was gone. What would a lawsuit have accomplished? I didn't need their money. I needed my child alive and well." He shook his head again. "You're wasting your time." He looked to Sarah then. "Avalon is the best in the country, maybe the world. They screen their employees better than the NSA vets their own."

"Then you won't mind giving us the names of any doctors or nurses involved with your daughter's care there," Tom prompted.

Adams stood. "I won't be a party to this waste of time. Avalon has an administrator who can assist you with this pointless endeavor."

Tom pushed to his feet and Sarah did the same. "Senator, I know this is difficult," she offered, "but—"

"That's what I find so stunning," Adams said, cutting her off. "I did my research on you, Detective. You do know, both of you, and still you're pursuing this nonsense." He glared at Tom then. "When I called Quantico for help, I didn't expect them to send the husband of the detective already working on the case. I'm certain this arrangement is less than ethical. I will be reaching out to your superior, Cuddahy."

"Do what you feel you must, Senator," Tom said. "Our only interest is in finding your daughter."

Adams gestured to the door of his study. "I'll show you out."

"Please let Mrs. Adams know we're working around the clock," Sarah said, in hopes of salvaging some connection with the man, as they moved into the entry hall.

For one moment, Sarah sensed she had reached beyond the senator's fury, and then he turned his back. "I'll tell her." Adams walked away, leaving them standing in the grand entry hall.

"I hope you know what you're doing," Sarah warned Tom before walking out.

The next interview was going to be conducted her way.

HOLY CROSS HOSPITAL
SILVER SPRINGS, MARYLAND, 7:49 P.M.

Lawrence Cashion listened as Tom explained why the FBI wanted to question him after the local police already had. The man insisted the strain of the police questioning coupled with the trauma of finding his wife and daughter missing had brought on the heart attack he'd suffered.

Sarah wouldn't deny the events of the past twelve or so hours had been horrifying for the man, but she'd also read the reports from the officers who had searched his home. Judging by the empty liquor bottle and the blood alcohol level he'd had when he showed up at the police precinct, his recent binge likely contributed to the problem as well.

Both his wife and daughter remained missing. The mother's disappearance was a significant deviation from the MO of the others in Sarah's investigation. As was the blood they had found at the scene. Cashion, or someone, had gone to great lengths to clean it up with bleach, but he'd failed to get it all. Something had happened in that home and Cashion wasn't talking.

The Cashion child was like the others. Her age, the fact she'd lost a sibling, and birthplace all fit the profile. Sarah was still on the fence with the genetic designer children or whatever business. The theory seemed too improbable. In her opinion, looking into any employees who had a grudge against Avalon or who just wanted to capitalize on an opportunity were the better scenarios.

Still, whatever else stood between her and Tom, he'd never been anything other than a topnotch investigator. For him to make that leap there had to be more he wasn't telling her. The whole need-to-know nonsense. If she didn't need to know, then why the hell were they working together?

"Mr. Cashion," Sarah said, "you stated that your wife took your daughter to a birthday party. Do you typically go to bed so early? We spoke with the Sims family and they're certain your wife and daughter left the party around eight. Since they live no more than twenty minutes away, your family should have been home by eight thirty."

"Like I told the detectives this morning," Cashion licked his visibly dry lips, "I've been working a lot of long hours lately. I crashed last night. Didn't know I was in the world until about eight this morning."

"Did your crash have anything to do with the amount of alcohol you consumed?" she prodded. He'd been asked about this already as well, but so far he hadn't admitted to having gone on a bender. He had no current record. If he'd ever had any legal trouble with alcohol it was not on his record.

"I've worked day and night for weeks to win the bid on an account that was stolen from me by a competitor. So, yes, I had a few drinks last night. What else do you want to hear? If you showed as much interest in finding my daughter and wife, maybe they'd be here with me now instead of God knows where!"

"Let's talk about your first daughter," Tom cut in smoothly, "the one who died the year before Cassie was born."

Cashion's face turned beet red. "I'm not saying anything else without my lawyer present."

Sarah's cell vibrated. While Tom attempted to placate the man she withdrew it from her jacket pocket and checked the screen. Larson. She stepped out of the room and accepted the call.

"You have something new for me?" Sarah held her breath. She prayed it wasn't another missing child.

"Nothing good," Larson said, his tone somber. "We found Mary Cashion's body. She was in the pond in the park north of her home. Cause of death appears to be head trauma. The evidence techs are comparing her blood to what was found in the house. I'm guessing they'll get a match. The lab's going over both the victim's car and the husband's. A uniform is headed your way to make sure Cashion stays put."

Sarah closed her eyes. Oh hell. "No sign of the little girl?"

"Not yet."

She blew out a breath. "I guess this means I get the unpleasant duty of telling Cashion his wife's body has been found."

"While you're at it you might suggest this would be a good time for him to start talking."

"Yeah." She somehow doubted that would happen. The man was already whining for his lawyer. "Thanks."

Tom stepped into the corridor. "He's done."

Sarah reached for the door. "I'm not."

"I told you I have nothing else to say!" Cashion ranted as she entered his room once more. He grabbed the call button. "I'm calling security."

"No need," Sarah assured him. "There will be a uniformed officer outside your door for the rest of your stay, Mr. Cashion."

His brow furrowed in question. "Am I in danger?"

His question gave her pause, but Sarah pressed on. "Sir, I'm sorry to have to tell you this, but your wife's body was found. This is a homicide investigation now. If there is anything about your previous statements you want to revise, I would suggest you do it now."

"What about my daughter?" Cashion snatched at the wires monitoring his heart and pulse rates as if he might jerk them loose and make a run for it. "Where's my daughter?" he screamed.

"Sir." Sarah held up her hands. "Your daughter is still missing. Only your wife's body was found."

Cashion dropped his head against the pillow and howled in agony.

Sarah touched his arm. He jerked, glared at her. "Mr. Cashion, your daughter still needs your help. Is there anything you want to tell me now that might help us find her?"

Cashion's face wilted. "I don't know. I blacked out. Woke up with blood all over my hands. Dear God." He squeezed his eyes shut. "I think I killed my wife."

By the time the uniform arrived Cashion had lapsed into sobs. Sarah reminded him of his rights and took his statement, for what it was worth. He had either killed his wife or he'd found her body and tried to hide it. For now, there was no way to know what happened.

As she and Tom exited the hospital silence hung between them. She climbed into the passenger side of his SUV. Like hers, Tom's vehicle had that lived in look. She imagined he spent as much time away from home as she did.

Why go home when there was nothing there to go home to?

"Why don't I take you to dinner?" he offered. "We both have to eat."

Since she hadn't eaten since grabbing a cup of yogurt on her way out the door this morning she could definitely eat. The trouble was she knew where spending time with him would lead. The same place it always took them—a screaming match.

"That's probably not a good idea. We should keep this about the case."

He hesitated before starting the engine. "You didn't do anything wrong, Sarah. When will you see that?"

Agony lashed through her. "Just take me to my car, Tom."

He pounded the steering wheel with his fist, startling her. "When will you stop blaming yourself? It's been five years!" He glared at her. "Our daughter is gone, but it's not your fault."

"I'll get a cab."

He grabbed her arm when she would have reached for the door. "I would have done the same thing if I'd been in your position. We both know it wasn't your fault."

His words were like scalding water pouring over her body. Emotion blurred her vision, had her heart swelling in her throat. "If I'd gone home on time, Sophie would have been with me. It *was* my fault." She shrugged off his touch.

"We, better than anyone, know how evil works. How the hell can you blame yourself for what some sick bastard did?"

"How the hell can you not hate me for not being home on time?" She shook with the agony charging through her now. "I waited and waited for you to show me what you really felt and you just kept holding it back. Instead, we walked around pretending. But I knew." She pounded her chest. "*I knew*! You hated me for what happened. Why can't you say it? Dammit! Just say it!"

He faced forward again. "I don't hate you, Sarah. I've never hated you. I hate the son of a bitch who did this to our family."

Sarah closed her eyes and fought to hold back the tears. He could pretend all he wanted to, but she knew the truth. Whether he ever said the words out loud or not, she knew he hated her.

She couldn't blame him.

She hated herself.

105 7TH STREET, WASHINGTON, D.C., 10:30 P.M.

Sarah stood in the entry hall of her home. She'd been standing here for twenty minutes or so. Her purse had slid down her shoulder and collapsed to the floor. She'd told herself repeatedly to move and somehow she couldn't.

This had been her home her entire life. As an only child she'd inherited the townhome when her father died while she was in college. Her mother had died when she was seven. Later, when she and Tom had gotten engaged, then married, they had decided to keep this place instead of selling and buying something new. The townhouse was huge, plenty large enough for raising a family. There was even a postage stamp sized backyard.

She could sell it now. Downsize and stash a nice chunk in savings. Homes in this area went for top dollar. The townhouse would easily go for a million and a half. She wouldn't have to walk past Sophie's bedroom anymore. She wouldn't have to block the memories of making love with Tom in her own bedroom.

There were advantages to starting fresh with a clean slate.

Except this was Sophie's home. If she was still alive, she might come back here one day. It happened. Abducted children, if they escaped or survived to adulthood, sometimes sought out their real parents once more—unless they'd been totally brainwashed into believing they were someone else.

Sophie *could* come back.

That was the sole reason Sarah endured the haunting memories. She had learned to walk through the house without seeing or hearing or feeling anything.

Spending the better part of the day with Tom had disabled her ability to block the images and sounds, like the way the front door squeaked when she closed it. Sophie used to laugh every time that sound echoed down the hall. The whisper of their bare feet on the wood floor. Leaving their shoes next to the table where mail and cell phones landed each evening had been habit.

Sarah closed her eyes. If she tried she could smell the scent of rain on her child's hair and skin. She and Sophie were the world's worst about forgetting their umbrellas. Street parking ensured they made many dashes through the rain and snow.

Even now, Tom's scent lingered inside Sarah, around her. He still used the same soap. It reminded her of all those times they had showered together, making love and wondering if they'd ever get pregnant again.

Sophie had been easy. They'd made the decision the time was right and suddenly Sarah was pregnant. Number two hadn't happened.

Then Sophie vanished.

Sarah shrugged out of her coat and let it fall to the floor with her purse. She toed off her shoes and started forward. She should eat. Shower. Take a pill and go to bed. No more thinking. No more seeing.

Slowly, she went through the steps. A can of chicken soup with crackers. A beer for washing down the pill she hated and loved at the same time. Then bed.

She climbed between the sheets and told her brain to shut down. No matter that Tom had not slept in this bed in more than fourteen months and twenty-nine days, she could smell him all around her. He had invaded her senses and would not be evicted.

The sound of Sophie giggling followed Sarah to sleep.

CHAPTER THIRTEEN

Her cell woke her. Sarah sat up, scrubbed a hand over her mouth before shoving the hair from her face. *Tom calling* flashed on her screen.

"What?" She reached for the bottle of water on her nightstand. Her mouth was dry as hell.

"We have an employee from Avalon who's come forward. He's agreed to a meeting. I'll pick you up in fifteen minutes."

"I'll drive my—" The call dropped and Sarah glared at her phone. Had he just hung up on her? Maybe he'd gotten another call.

"Dammit."

She did not want to ride with him, but if he'd landed a lead she wanted to be a part of it. She desperately needed a break in this case.

Ten minutes later, as promised, Tom's SUV eased to the curb behind her car. Sarah stepped outside, set the alarm and locked the door, then hustled down to the sidewalk. Tom reached across the console and passenger seat to open the door for her. She climbed in and fastened her seatbelt.

"Where're we going?" She reminded herself to relax. Maybe she should have taken the time to finish her coffee.

"He wants to keep his cooperation under the radar so we're meeting at an IHOP."

"How did he know to contact you?"

"I've been putting out feelers for a while now," he explained without explaining anything at all. "Patrick Schneider was a maintenance engineer at Avalon. Two weeks ago he was fired. I guess he has an ax to grind now that he's been let go."

"A grudge makes him an unreliable source," she reminded the man who'd been doing this longer than her. She'd turned thirty-seven last month, which made Tom forty. She couldn't deny that he'd always been good at his job. No matter, this whole situation just didn't feel right.

"We have nothing to lose by hearing what he has to say."

Now there was something they could agree on. They had nothing to lose.

IHOP, Baltimore Avenue
College Park, Maryland, 5:09 a.m.

"People pay big money for the doctors at Avalon," Schneider said. He glanced around the nearly deserted restaurant before hunching his shoulders around his head as he leaned forward. "They do things no one else does."

Tom sensed the tension in Sarah. She wasn't buying his story any more than she had the one Tom had given her less than twenty-four hours ago. He didn't blame her. If he hadn't seen the undeniable evidence in that small, quiet Tennessee town last year, he wouldn't have believed it himself. But it was real. At least one cloned human had survived to adulthood. Unimaginable genetic experiments had been conducted on so many others.

Paul Phillips and his family had barely escaped with their lives. Their secret was one the world could never know. Tom had ensured any files on Paul's wife and sister-in-law vanished. As deep as his loyalty to the Bureau went, his loyalty to the people he cared about went much deeper. He just hoped Sarah would forgive him one day for what he'd done in his efforts to help her.

"You need to be more specific, Mr. Schneider," Sarah pressed. "What you've said so far is public knowledge. Avalon is one of the most renowned private hospitals in the country. The facility didn't reach that status without world-class physicians. No law against being the best."

Schneider glanced around again. He was nervous. No doubt about it. He'd been waiting at the booth in the very back corner of the dining room when they arrived. His head hadn't stopped oscillating since.

"If they find out I looked at the charts…" His eyes went wide with fear. "They'll kill me."

"What charts?" Tom asked, careful to keep his voice down. Though there was only one other couple in the restaurant, there were plenty of waitresses preparing for the morning rush.

"The charts of certain patients." Schneider cleared his throat. "Rich kids. The parents brought them there when nothing else worked."

"Were these children ill?" Sarah asked. There was a fine tremor in her hand as she reached for her coffee.

She wasn't as strong as she wanted Tom to believe. God almighty, he was worried about her. This case had consumed his existence for more than a year. Still, he should have made time to check on her. No wonder she was determined to go through with this divorce.

Schneider nodded. "Most of them died."

"Doesn't sound as if those award winning physicians did anything special if the children died anyway," Sarah suggested.

"I don't know about that, but I know what I saw in those charts."

"What was that, Mr. Schneider?" Tom was ready to hear more than speculation. If the man had something concrete he needed to spit it out.

"The kids weren't listed as patients. They were listed by number as *test specimens.*"

Tom looked toward the waitress. It was time to make this guy put up or shut up. "I don't appreciate my time being wasted, Mr. Schneider."

Schneider surveyed the restaurant again to make sure the waitress wasn't coming. "If I tell you more, I don't want my name in it. I don't trust these guys."

"Why?" Sarah asked. "Why would you be afraid of anyone at the hospital?"

"Those kids were in a special unit at the hospital." Schneider leaned across the table again, his voice getting lower with each word spoken. "None of the regular staff goes in there. The patients don't go in the usual way. They don't go out the usual way either. If someone dies in that unit an unmarked van takes the body away. And I don't mean someone from one of the funeral homes. I know all those guys." He looked from Sarah to Tom and back. "This is different."

"Why come forward with this information now?" Sarah asked. "You've worked there for a decade. What happened to prompt you to speak up now?"

That would have been Tom's next question. This guy wasn't telling them everything he knew. He was holding back some relevant piece of information.

"That missing kid, Myers, he was…" He moistened his lips. Cleared his throat again. "He was in the unit and his parents took him out. There was a big hubbub about it. The next thing I knew he was on the news."

Sarah glanced at Tom, and then asked, "You're certain? Sean Myers?"

Schneider nodded. "I swear to God. I don't know about the other kids, but I believe with all my heart Avalon had something to do with that boy going missing."

"In ten years, you never noticed activities out of the ordinary until now?" The revelation was stunning, no question. It was the man's motive for coming forward that worried Tom.

"I'm human." Schneider shrugged. "Avalon paid the bills. I looked the other way when I saw anything a little off. I don't have any reason to look the other way now."

"Give us one good reason," Sarah proposed, "we should take the word of a disgruntled former employee?"

Another shrug. "It's the truth. I don't need a reason to tell the truth."

"Maybe we'd be a little more convinced if you shared a few more examples of situations where you looked the other way." Tom needed more than supposition. The story had him chomping at the bit to look more deeply into Avalon. Moving forward with caution was essential considering all they had was the word of a man who'd recently been fired and the fact that Tom wasn't exactly in a good place with his superiors right now.

"That's all I got. Lots of situations I encountered felt wrong, but this is the only time I can point to a specific wrongdoing. That kid was a patient in Avalon one day and suddenly he was on the news the next. That has to mean something. If it does, maybe I'll win one of those rewards."

Each of the families was offering a reward for information leading to the discovery of their child. According to Sarah, the rewards had brought out the desperate, the greedy, and at least a few nut cases. No true leads.

Whatever this guy's story, his sudden compulsion likely had more to do with the rewards and wanting to get back at his ex-employer than a sense of doing the right thing.

Tom passed Schneider his card. "Call me if you think of anything else."

"Whatever else you do," Schneider said, "you should check out that hospital. They're doing bad things to kids. Believe that if you believe nothing else."

When Schneider had gone, Sarah moved around to the other side of the booth. "If what he says about Sean Myers is true, considering all eight children were born at that hospital, I say there's a connection. We should go back to the parents and push for answers."

Tom reached for one of the menus the waitress had left when she'd taken their coffee order. "We should eat."

"We should get out there and start pounding on doors," she argued.

"Too early." He checked the screen of his cell. "We eat. We give them time to have coffee, and then we go pound on doors."

"I'm not hungry."

There was a lot he could say to that, but he knew better. Strong-arm tactics didn't work with Sarah. He'd learned that the hard way. "I am."

He placed his order, making sure to go big so he could share in case she changed her mind. To his surprise, she ordered a scrambled egg with a piece of wheat toast.

When the waitress was gone, Tom ventured. "I hear you made lieutenant."

"I did." She freshened her coffee, took a sip.

He glanced out at the sky. "Looks like rain."

"Hmm-Mmm."

"I like your hair," he dared to say. She glanced up and he smiled no matter that she didn't. "It's longer. I haven't seen it that long since we first met."

She tucked a handful behind her ear. "I've been too busy to get to the salon. I usually keep it in a ponytail, but I was in a hurry this morning."

"I like it down." He'd always loved her hair, even when it was much shorter. The deep, rich brown was a vivid contrast to her smooth pale skin. She reminded him of a porcelain doll, precious and fragile. He had wanted to protect her, but she'd shown him that she was strong and brave and didn't need protecting. Yet, losing Sophie had stolen some part of her he couldn't quite name. She still did her job and did it well from all reports. He had to give her credit there, but there was something missing. The fire was gone from her eyes, he decided.

He'd changed, too. His life revolved around work as well. His apartment was nothing more than a hotel room. He couldn't care less where he laid his head to sleep. Work was his life. The rest of the time he basically existed.

How the hell would they ever get beyond this painful place?

"So Phillips is okay?" she asked tentatively. She met his eyes for a mere second.

"He's good. He's married and they have a… child." She flinched when he said the last. Why hadn't he left out the part about the kid? Paul Phillips had tried to help when Sophie disappeared, but he'd been too far gone in his own misery to pull himself together. Tom might have hated him for that except he'd understood Paul hadn't been mentally or physically capable of doing more. Sarah, on the other hand, hadn't seen it that way.

"That's nice." She stared at her coffee some more. "I'm happy things worked out for him."

"I'm glad you kept the house."

Another quick glance his way. "Why would I sell? My parents would want me to keep the house."

He decided not to say anything about the peeling paint or the overgrown landscape. Like him she worked all the time. Home maintenance was likely the last thing on her mind. The realization that those were things he should be taking care of punched him in the gut, but he wasn't welcome in the home they'd once shared. Not since the day he'd hauled her out of the house and had her committed to a facility where she would get the help she needed.

He doubted she would ever forgive him for taking that step. He couldn't blame her really. He'd fallen down on the role of good husband in a hundred different ways. He should've handled things differently. Too late to repair that bridge now it seemed.

"You're right." He reached for his coffee. "It's a great house."

Sarah suddenly looked at him as if she'd just remembered some terrible thing she'd forgotten to say. "I don't even know where you live."

"I guess that's why the divorce papers were served at the office." He forced a smile. "I thought I sent you the address." He distinctly remembered calling and leaving a message.

"Maybe you did."

Their order arrived, preventing the need for further small talk. They ate in silence. She muddled through the egg and toast. He goaded her into a bite of pancake. She actually smiled once and he felt fairly certain it was real. He'd glimpsed the tiniest sparkle in those brown eyes of hers he had always loved.

A final cup of coffee and Tom felt almost human. "Do you remember the last time we were at an IHOP?" They'd been on the way to Boston to his cousin's wedding. Sophie had...

Agony claimed Sarah's face. "We should go." She grabbed her jacket and purse and scooted from the booth.

Tom felt like kicking himself. Was there anything they could talk about that their daughter wouldn't be a part of? Oh yeah, right. Work. The case.

Outside the restaurant, Sarah hesitated to take a call. He hit the remote to start his SUV and get the heat going. It was cold as hell for October. Maybe winter was coming early this year.

Sarah ended the call and gave him an address. "We may have a lead on Cashion's wife."

The children were Tom's top priority, but Mary Cashion deserved justice, too. If her murder helped find her daughter and the rest of the children alive, maybe her death wouldn't be for naught.

CHAPTER FOURTEEN

Smithsonian 10th Street, Washington, D.C., 8:00 a.m.

"The world has no idea the secrets we keep."

Joe Adams didn't give a damn about the world's secrets. "Where is she?"

Dr. Detlef Meltzer gazed upon the Genome exhibit as if it were a god.

Joe was grateful the museum wasn't open because he was on the verge of losing it. He'd spent the past forty or so hours hanging onto his sanity by a damned thread. His wife was at home sedated. Late last night when he'd called Chief Larson and demanded an update, he'd learned something Detective Cuddahy had opted to keep from him. Agent Cuddahy had suggested to Larson that there was reason to believe the missing children had been subjected to unethical medical experiments at Avalon.

He'd tried several times to get in touch with Meltzer after learning all the missing children had been born at Avalon. It wasn't until Joe had left the message that the FBI was on to him that Meltzer had returned his call. If this bastard had anything to do with Katie's disappearance…

Meltzer settled his arrogant attention on Joe. "There are few things in life as precious to us as our children. Rare is the woman or the man who wouldn't readily die for his or her offspring."

Adams moved into the doctor's personal space. "Where is she?"

"We have a binding contract, Senator." Meltzer inclined his head and studied Joe as if he were one of his lab rats. "You are never to speak of our arrangement under any circumstances."

Fury pounded in Joe's veins. All that prevented him from beating the hell out of this man right now was the knowledge that he would not gain anything by doing so. Without doubt the move would ensure he lost his daughter forever. "I have kept our damned bargain. I fulfilled my end. Why the hell did you take my daughter and the others? If you hurt my baby…"

"Paranoia is a powerful force. I suspect that, as well as fear, is skewing your judgment just now, *Senator* Adams. Otherwise you would see how foolish your accusations sound."

Joe grappled to hang onto his composure. "All those missing children were born at your facility, Meltzer. With the FBI talking about unethical experiments, you think I don't know what that means?"

Meltzer smiled. "Hundreds of children are born at Avalon each year. As for the FBI, it's always overdramatizing when facing failure. However, I'm confident you will enlighten me as to your thoughts on their allegations."

"Something's gone wrong with your test group. You're the one who's paranoid and afraid, so you're taking steps to destroy the evidence." Joe pointed a finger at the man he had once considered a genius and his savior. "You told me the shaking and the sleep walking were nothing to worry about. You told me Katie would be fine."

"If you had proof of your suspicions I'm certain we wouldn't be having this conversation just now. You would be telling your friends at the FBI. Why aren't you, Senator Adams? After all, your child is missing. Are you so afraid of your constituents finding out who you really are that you would allow your daughter to suffer instead?"

Joe grabbed him by the labels. The two body-guards who followed Meltzer around waiting to do his bidding came to attention. Meltzer waved them off.

"You bring my daughter back to me and we'll forget this ever happened."

Meltzer pushed Joe's hands away. "Pull yourself together, Senator."

Joe glanced around, tried to shake off his fury. This bastard had his little girl, Joe was certain of it. All he wanted was Katie. "I want her back. Now. Unharmed."

"I assure you she is unharmed."

Relief swept through him, had his knees trying to buckle.

"Certain issues have cropped up that I must attend to before returning the children."

The lump of emotion in his throat made speaking near impossible. "She's going to be all right, isn't she?"

Meltzer smiled. "Of course. She's perfect. As soon as this matter is resolved, the children will be returned to their homes safe and sound and no one will be the wiser as to the necessity of their absence."

"Are all the children suffering from some issue?"

"Nothing I can't handle, I assure you."

Joe was just desperate enough to believe him. "Why wasn't this handled in the clinic like before?" When Katie was two she'd slipped into a coma for no apparent reason. Three days later she'd been fine.

"There is a man who threatens all we've attained, Joe. He would stop me and destroy what the world will never see as real children. For that reason, I was forced to take extreme measures."

A new kind of fury slammed Joe. "Who is this man?" His Katie was as real as any child. They had gone to a great deal of trouble to ensure she was as genetically perfect as possible. No inherited risk of cancer or heart disease or any of the other big killers. Their child had been given every possible advantage.

"This FBI agent, Tom Cuddahy, who has you up in arms. He is determined to stop my work. If the world learns of our accomplishments they won't understand. They're not ready. We mustn't allow Cuddahy to interfere. At my age, I wouldn't survive long in prison. I dare say there would be no hope for poor little Katie then. I'm the only one who can help her when issues arise."

"I'll take care of Cuddahy." Joe's jaw ached from clinching his teeth so hard.

"I hope we're not too late," Meltzer asserted. "His efforts could destabilize the entire program. The children could potentially die horrific deaths without my careful oversight."

"Whatever I have to do," Joe assured him. "I will get Cuddahy out of here. When can Katie come home?"

"You took care of the other?"

"The vote will go our way, no question."

Meltzer patted Joe on the shoulder. Joe flinched. "Then all is well."

"Why didn't you tell me you needed to see Katie? We've always cooperated fully and brought her in for any needed appointments."

"As I said, Agent Cuddahy left me no choice."

"But the children are safe?" Joe countered, needing confirmation.

"The children are quite safe. You'll see for yourself soon."

"When can I speak to her?" Joe needed to hear his baby's voice.

"I'm afraid that would only make things more difficult for Katie," Meltzer insisted. "She'll be back home before you know it."

Joe told himself to relax. "You'll keep me informed?"

Meltzer gave a single nod. "I will."

"I can assure my wife our daughter is going to be fine?"

"As long as you take care of Agent Cuddahy, all the children will be fine."

"I'll take care of him," Joe promised again. "I'll do that today."

Meltzer turned his attention back to the exhibit. "So fascinating. It's a shame the creator arrived at so few accurate conclusions."

Joe tried to laugh, but the sound came out more like a strangled cough. He wanted to be relieved, but he was too damned scared. "I'll contact you as soon as it's done."

"No need. I have people who are watching the FBI's activities. I'll be informed when he is no longer an issue."

"Tell my daughter I love her."

"Of course." Meltzer smiled reassuringly, yet Joe found no comfort in the gesture.

Joe left the meeting and actually made it to his car before breaking down. Then he laid his forehead against the steering wheel and he sobbed.

He was terrified Meltzer was lying.

CHAPTER FIFTEEN

Sarah watched Dwight West carefully as he considered how to answer her question. The PI was a large man who likely intimidated most people. His heavily muscled build told her that the gym was one of his favorite hangouts. On the way here, she'd run a quick background check. He had never been in any real trouble. A couple of run-ins with ex-husbands and ex-boyfriends of clients, but charges had always been dismissed before a court appearance.

West had established his business in the DC area ten years ago. Prior to that he'd worked with a partner down in New Orleans. His face bore the scars of more than a few battles. Despite the war wounds and minor brushes with the law he had a solid reputation. His website was loaded with what appeared to be legit testimonials from clients. Considering he'd been willing to come to his office on a Sunday morning to answer their questions, Sarah figured he was pretty decent guy.

"I spoke to Mary Cashion on Friday morning." He leaned back in his chair. "She was leaving her husband." West reached into his desk and removed a large padded envelope. "She paid me for a new identity." He held on to the envelope, his gaze resting on Tom. "Some people believe creating alternative IDs for a situation like this is a crime. You one of 'em, Agent Cuddahy?"

"We're here about Mary Cashion's murder and her missing daughter." Tom shrugged. "Your assistance is greatly appreciated. We have no interest in your other activities unless they relate to missing or exploited children."

"I guess we're on the same page then." He tossed the envelope to Sarah. "Lawrence Cashion has been abusing his wife for fifteen years."

Sarah studied the passports and other papers West had created or purchased. "This is very good work."

"My clients pay me well. Only the best will do."

Sarah tucked the documents back into the envelope and placed it on his desk. "She was so afraid of her husband she felt it necessary to have a new identity?" Lawrence Cashion had no record. His wife apparently never reported the abuse. It pained Sarah to hear stories like this. Didn't matter that she'd been a cop for more than a decade, the helplessness, fear, and suffering of women like Mary Cashion still got to her. There needed to be better, more efficient ways to protect abused women. And the children…the thought twisted like a knife in her side. Anyone who harmed a child deserved to be slaughtered.

West nodded. "She'd tried to leave him before. He always brought her back." He made a face, and then flared his hands. "Look, she said he beat her up from time to time—always below the neck. Never any broken bones or concussions, she claimed. But," he hesitated, "this is just my gut instinct, I think he killed their first child, Catherine."

Sarah's heart rate picked up as her own instincts started to hum. "The report on Catherine Cashion's death says she fell down the stairs."

"She was autistic," Tom added. "According to her health records she had a habit of injuring herself."

"Asperger Syndrome," West corrected. "She was a brilliant kid with the occasional violent episodes. That's the way it works sometimes. Yeah, she beat her head against the wall a time or two when she got angry. Threw things. That's not uncommon. Throwing herself down the stairs is not so common."

"You sound as if you're familiar with the problem," Sarah commented.

"My son has Asperger Syndrome. He's sixteen and life is hell sometimes. Yeah, I know a little something about it."

"Other than your personal experience," Tom redirected, "did Mrs. Cashion say anything that led you to believe Cashion was responsible for their daughter's death?"

"She said plenty. Danced all around it. Trouble is, I don't think she actually witnessed the incident.

I think she heard the screaming, heard the fall, then saw her husband at the top of the stairs and her daughter crumpled at the bottom. She never said he pushed the child. What she said was she didn't want to wait until something bad happened again. What does that tell you?"

"A great deal," Sarah agreed. "Is there anything else she spoke of, maybe related to Cassie? As you know, we're desperate to find her." And the others.

"She was a lot more vague about their youngest. She mentioned she had to protect her. That she was special."

When the PI fell silent, Tom prodded, "Nothing else? No explanation of what she meant by special?"

West shook his head. "I hate this shit, you know." He heaved another sigh. "I do what I can, but sometimes it's just not enough. If that kid is dead, too, I'm gonna feel guilty about it the rest of my life."

"Why is that? From what I see, you were doing all you could to help." Sarah certainly understood some level of regret even when you did your best.

"She wanted to leave on Friday while her husband thought she and her daughter were at a birthday party. Get a couple hours' head start, but she had to wait." He gestured to the envelope. "That stuff didn't come in until yesterday morning. By then it was too late."

The idea that Mary Cashion had been that close to escaping sickened Sarah. She stood. "Thank you, Mr. West. We may need to call on you again."

He pushed out of his chair and looked from Sarah to Tom. "I want you to get this guy. Anything I can do, I'm there."

Frustration hammered at Sarah as she and Tom exited the building. Setting it aside wasn't so easy. Put together the tidbit Schneider had given them and the story West had provided and they had basically nothing. The information presented a certain insight, but no direction. No true lead.

The chilly wind whipped around her, making her shiver. Despite the wind the sun was bright this morning. Sarah wished she'd remembered her sunglasses.

In her opinion, the only potential follow-up in front of them just now was Avalon. What was the real connection between these children and that hospital? Why these children in particular? Was a deceased sibling part of the criteria? Seemed too strong a connection to be coincidence, though for the life of her she couldn't see it.

"Are we interviewing Cashion again?" she asked as they reached Tom's SUV. That would be her next move.

"Cashion had his interview." Tom opened the passenger side door for her. "This time he gets an interrogation."

Sarah settled into the seat and waited for Tom to get in on the other side. "The man did just have a heart attack." Not that she had any sympathy, particularly after their talk with West.

"If he killed his wife and daughter," Tom started the engine, "he's going to wish that heart attack had done more than land him in the hospital."

Sarah told herself to look away, but somehow she couldn't. She hadn't allowed herself to look directly at Tom any more than absolutely necessary and then not for more than a fleeting second or two. It hurt too much. Every time their eyes met she saw Sophie. Even now she wanted to look away, to make that thread of ever present pain subside, and she couldn't.

Thirteen months, one week and three days had passed since they'd seen each other. Funny how she remembered the exact date of all their lasts—last time they slept together, last time they saw each other…last time they saw their daughter. Tom had tried repeatedly to mend the rift after having her committed. He would show up at her door and she would refuse to talk to him or even to open the door.

Finally, she'd stopped answering the phone as well and he'd given up.

There were lines around his eyes and mouth that hadn't been there before. If she looked really closely she was fairly certain there was a scattering of gray in his dark hair. He looked leaner than before. And tired. He looked so very tired.

The last five years had taken a visible toll on both of them. Had he cried himself to sleep as many nights as she had? Did he still wake up thinking Sophie would come bouncing into the room smiling and chattering the way she always had? Was he totally numb ninety-nine percent of the time the way Sarah was? Or had someone else given him what she no longer could?

An ache pierced her. Why didn't he just sign the damned divorce papers? All she wanted was to…

To what? Move on? Impossible. Put the past completely behind her? That was never going to happen despite her best efforts. Her entire existence was about work and not looking back.

He glanced her way. She whipped her attention forward.

"You can ask me anything you want." He braked for a turn. "I'll answer."

"Who said I had any questions?" Her rapid pulse and the ache in her chest said plenty, but she intended to keep that to herself.

"I've known you since you were a freshman in college." He glanced at her again. "I know your every expression, Sarah. You have questions."

"You haven't known me in a long time, Tom." It hurt to say his name. She blinked at the foolish moisture that gathered in her eyes. She never said his name…never said their child's—not out loud. "People change."

"Why don't I give you the answers I think you want?"

His arrogance irritated her. "Did your old friend teach you mind reading, too?" His silence deflated her irritation in one fell swoop. How the hell could he still affect her so—make her want to rethink her strategy for survival? "Give it your best shot."

Another fleeting slant of those green eyes arrowed in her direction. "There's no one else, Sarah."

She hugged her arms around herself. "That's too bad."

More silence. It went on so long she decided she'd gotten her point across, but then he sighed, a weary, aching sound.

"I dream about you—both of you—most nights."

He smiled sadly. She shouldn't have looked, but she did.

"It's crazy, I know. Sometimes I rouse, and in that moment between asleep and awake, I can hear her voice. She wants to take Sam outside. You're telling her she has to wait until after breakfast." He tried to laugh, but a catch in his voice disrupted the sound. "Sometimes I can smell her shampoo. I'd kiss her head and there was that sweet fragrance from the—"

"Johnson's Kids Strawberry Sensation." Sarah hugged herself tighter and bit her lip to keep it from trembling. There was nothing she could do to stem the burn in her eyes.

He stopped for a traffic light and faced her. "Sometimes, as I drift off to sleep, I can feel you touching me...I can taste your lips."

She tried to look away. She really did, but she couldn't. She couldn't breathe or speak. She could only stare into his eyes...*Sophie's eyes.*

A horn blared behind them.

He shifted his attention to the street and drove.

Some part of her wished they could just keep driving…until they escaped the horrible nightmare that was their lives.

HOLY CROSS HOSPITAL
SILVER SPRINGS, MARYLAND, 12:55 P.M.

"I hope we're not interrupting anything," Tom announced as he and Sarah entered Cashion's room.

"Let me call you back." Cashion ended the call and laid his cell phone carefully on the portable table extended across the bed. "Have you found my daughter?"

"No, Mr. Cashion, we haven't." Tom braced his hands on his hips, pushing aside the lapels of his jacket to ensure his credentials and weapon were on display. He wanted the man intimidated. "As a matter of fact, we were hoping you could help us with that."

Cashion shook his head. "I don't know anything. I told you, I can't remember. The last thing I remember is Mary and Cassie leaving for the birthday party. There's nothing after that." He shuddered. "Not until I woke up with blood on my hands."

"Did you try to clean up the blood, Mr. Cashion?" Sarah asked.

He nodded. "I was scared. I tried to clean it up, then took a shower."

"At any time while you were doing all this cleaning," Tom pressed, his fingers itching to shake the bastard, "did you stop and consider where your daughter was?"

Cashion glared at him. "Of course I did. I searched the whole house. I couldn't find her. She must have seen what happened," he made a soft keening sound, "and ran away." He shook his head. "I would never hurt my daughter. Never."

"You wouldn't push her down the stairs if she made you angry?"

Cashion's face went deathly pale. "I didn't hurt Catherine. That was an accident."

"Was it?" Sarah argued. "You never hit Catherine the way you did Mary?"

"I never hit my wife! Who said such a thing?"

"You did hit your wife," Tom challenged. "You abused her for years. Her statements about your abuse are documented."

Cashion blinked once, twice. "I never hurt my daughters. Never."

"How can you be so sure, Mr. Cashion?" Sarah argued. "What about the blackouts? You said yourself this wasn't the first time."

His lips trembled. "I didn't hurt either of my daughters."

"Tell us what happened to Catherine," Sarah urged, her voice gentler now.

"Mary and I had been fighting. Catherine woke up and started screaming. I went upstairs and tried to calm her down, but she just kept getting more and more hysterical. Finally, I gave up. I was going to take her downstairs to her mother when she suddenly bolted away from me. I tried to grab her, but…" He started to sob. "She fell all the way to the bottom of the stairs."

"Did Cassie have an accident, too?" Tom demanded. He had no sympathy for the bastard. "Is that why you had to kill your wife? Two children dying in separate freak accidents would be a little difficult to explain."

"I swear," Cashion wailed, "I would never hurt my child."

Sarah held up her hands. "You know what, Mr. Cashion." He stared at her. "I believe you. I don't think you hurt either of your daughters."

"That's why I'm here," Tom warned him, "to keep the detective from overlooking the truth. I don't believe you for a second. I think you murdered both your daughters and when your wife threatened to call the police, you killed her, too."

Fear clouded the man's expression. "My daughter is missing and you're wasting time with these interrogation tactics!"

"Maybe your daughter's disappearance has something to do with Avalon," Sarah suggested, staying in good-cop mode. "We have seven others missing who were born at that hospital. Maybe they even killed your wife to get to your daughter."

Cashion's eyes widened. "What're you talking about?"

"You don't watch the news?" Tom shook his head. "For a mover and shaker like you, that's hard to believe."

"Are you referring to the children who've gone missing the past couple of weeks?" He turned his attention back to Sarah. "All those kids were born at Avalon?"

Sarah nodded. "You see what I mean? I believe there's a connection."

Something new flashed in the man's eyes. "Are you investigating the hospital?"

Tom had a hunch. "We are. We told the administrator that we were following up on the leads you provided?"

"What?" Sheer terror danced in his eyes then.

"You have some reason to be afraid of the hospital's administrator, Mr. Cashion?" Sarah asked.

"You don't understand," Cashion grabbed his cell phone as if he feared he might need to call for help, "we signed a nondisclosure statement. I can't talk about it. You have to leave now."

"The others are already talking," Tom lied. "Senator Adams is pushing hard for us to get to the bottom of what Avalon has done."

Tiny beads of sweat glistened on Cashion's face. "We were desperate."

Tom exchanged a knowing look with Sarah. She placed her hand over one of Cashion's to comfort him. He flinched. "Losing a child is devastating."

Cashion nodded. "They did everything they could at the ER." He cleared his throat. "But Catherine's neck was broken. They couldn't save her."

"She died here," Tom said, "in this ER."

Another weary nod from Cashion. "A man came into the room. We thought it was another of the doctors, but he wasn't on staff here."

"He had a proposition for you?" Tom prompted.

"He said he was sorry for our loss." Cashion looked from Tom to Sarah. "Then he asked what we would be willing to give to have our daughter back. Not another child. Not someone who looked like Catherine… *Catherine.*"

Sarah gasped, but she covered it well with a cough.

"How did he propose to do this?" Tom prepared for the part of this mystery he'd been expecting to unfold. They were close. He could feel it.

"He said they would take genetic material from Catherine before her body was taken away and then they would… *clone* her. Mary would carry her just as she'd carried her the first time." His lips spread into a smile even as the tears slid down his face. "She looked exactly like Catherine when she was born. Everything, from her first word to her first step was exactly the same. Except for the Asperger. They took care of that problem. Cassie is perfect."

Tom looked to Sarah, but she didn't appear ready to ask the next question. He pushed on. "You're saying they created an exact replica of your daughter?"

Cashion nodded. "Yes. Lately she'd even been remembering things she couldn't possibly have known, and yet, somehow she did." He shrugged. "Meltzer couldn't explain that one. She surprised us all with her knowledge of things that happened… *before*." Another wobbly smile. "They kept their promise. They gave us Catherine back."

Tom suspected the doctor at Avalon understood precisely what was happening. More of those random errors. "We need the name of the doctor who gave you your second daughter."

"We were forced to agree to never divulge anything about this," Cashion went on. "Mary and I assumed there were other families who went through the same program, but we never knew who they were." He frowned. "So all those missing children…?"

"The name," Tom pushed. "We need his name."

"Dr. Detlef Meltzer. The program was his brainchild."

Meltzer wasn't the name Tom had expected to hear. He'd been certain Avalon's administrator was the one.

"Did you ever speak to anyone else besides Meltzer?" Sarah asked.

"Even if there was a tech or nurse involved, Meltzer conducted all the procedures." Cashion closed his eyes. "Please. I can't talk about this anymore."

Tom disconnected the landline from the wall and dismantled Cashion's cell phone, tossing the SIM card into the cup of water on the bedside table. "You are not to speak of this conversation with anyone," he warned.

Cashion looked startled.

"To catch this guy and to find the children, he can't know we're on to him. We need the element of surprise." Tom needed Cashion to understand those terms.

"You think he has my daughter and the others? But why?"

"One of the children has developed a serious illness," Sarah explained.

"There are other things," Tom added. "Like your daughter's memories. Those kinds of unexpected developments could reveal to the rest of the world what Meltzer has been up to. There are laws against human cloning, Mr. Cashion. We have reason to believe, he's scrambling to do damage control."

"You're saying he may try to…destroy the children?"

Tom nodded. "That's what I'm saying."

The only thing he couldn't say right now was how he would stop this travesty.

CHAPTER SIXTEEN

Holy Cross Hospital,
Silver Springs, Maryland 10:00 p.m.

Lawrence Cashion awoke from a fitful sleep. His room was dark. Had he turned off the television? Maybe a nurse had come into the room without him waking.

He swiped a hand over his face and licked his lips. His mouth was so dry. He wished Mary were here. She would take care of him the way she always did. She knew how to make him feel better. But Mary was gone.

Had he killed her?

A moan rose in his throat. Surely, he hadn't gone that far? And his sweet baby girl? Had he harmed Cassie, too?

He squeezed his eyes shut and prayed. If there was a God in heaven would he have allowed Lawrence to do such heinous things?

Sobs choked him. He was all alone now. He had nothing.

"Why oh why, Lord?"

"That's very good question, Lawrence."

His eyes flew open. The room was completely dark…but he knew that voice. "What're you doing here, Meltzer?" Fury tightened his lips.

"Why, Lawrence, after all I've done for you and your family, how could you let me down so?"

Fear slid through him, making his diseased heart thump harder. "I don't know what you're talking about." He should have known he couldn't trust that cop and the FBI agent to keep his secret. They'd screwed him. *God, I don't want to die.*

The bastard laughed at him. "Ah, but you do know what I'm talking about, Lawrence. You failed to adhere to our contract. You failed your family. You've been talking to the FBI."

Agony howled through Lawrence. It was true. It was true. He'd failed everyone, including himself.

Meltzer's firm hand patted him on the shoulder. Lawrence jerked at the touch.

"There, there, Lawrence, no need to fall to pieces. We both know what must be done."

"What about the officer watching my room?" Would Meltzer kill him with a cop right outside? His heart pounded erratically.

The doctor smiled down at him. "No need to worry about him, Lawrence. I've had someone watching you. I grew concerned when Agent Cuddahy and Detective Cuddahy returned for a second interview and then a guard was placed at your door. I'm afraid that last cup of coffee won't keep him awake as he'd hoped. He's fast asleep. So you see, Lawrence, no one knows I'm here. If you do the right thing, perhaps I can find a new and better home for your sweet Cassie."

Lawrence didn't bother arguing. At least his little girl would be safe. He didn't even put up a struggle as the needle pierced his skin. He closed his eyes and waited for death. This was what he deserved.

Forgive me, Mary.

CHAPTER SEVENTEEN

2569 EDGE COVE ROAD
SAINT MICHAELS, MARYLAND, 11:50 P.M.

Sarah wanted to shake Tom, but she didn't dare touch him. They were wasting time. Cashion had named Meltzer. They should be questioning him right now instead of sitting here watching his house.

Once they'd located the doctor's home and started their surveillance, she had done some research on the man. Dr. Detlef Meltzer was seventy and a renowned geneticist. Meltzer's father, now deceased, left Germany as a young man in 1947 when Meltzer was just a toddler. The family settled in Boston. A Harvard Medical School graduate, Meltzer did his internship and residency at the prestigious Johns Hopkins University Hospital. The man was touted as a genius in the field of genetic research.

At fifty-two, he'd resigned as a distinguished professor of genetics and began a small, exclusive private practice with hospital privileges at Avalon. Six years ago he closed his practice. If Cashion could be believed, Meltzer had taken his work to an entirely new and completely unethical, as well as illegal, level. Confirming Cashion's story and finding where the illegal activities were taking place—and hopefully where the children were being held—was what they needed now.

The sticking point was that everything Sarah had been able to dig up so far suggested Detlef Meltzer was a model citizen. He spent a great deal of time supporting charities. Never had so much as a parking ticket. No malpractice suits. No debt. No tax issues. The possibility that they were wasting their time was immense. They had been watching the house since shortly before five this afternoon. Meltzer had only arrived home half an hour ago. He'd parked in the garage and there had been no activity outside the house since.

Sarah's patience was thinning. "What now?"

"We've been over this already," Tom said, his attention fixed on the luxurious home sprawled on two acres along the shore of the river. "If Meltzer senses we're on to him the children's lives could be in danger. We have to be patient."

"That's assuming he's our man." Sarah wanted to find those children and sitting here wasn't getting that done. "All we have to go on is the word of a suspected murderer." She had barely kept the anxiety at bay the past few hours. It was clawing hard at her now.

"Avalon is the common denominator. Cashion's statement merely confirms what I already suspected."

They'd stopped agreeing on how to conduct this investigation between the meeting with Schneider at IHOP and the interrogation of Cashion at Holy Cross. When she'd asked Tom why there weren't other agents working this case, he had blown her off and changed the subject. She might have dismissed his elusiveness as more of that need-to-know business except he wouldn't meet her eyes when he answered. That was usually her evasive tactic, for totally different reasons. Not Tom. He was always the forthright one. Her instincts warned there was something more keeping him quiet.

"Since I'm on the outside looking in," Sarah tried a different approach, "obviously I can't see the connection as well as you do."

"There are things I can't explain just yet."

"Got it. You do things based on what you know." Enough with the cloak and dagger routine. She grabbed her purse. "I do the same. I'll find my own way back home." She reached for the door handle.

"Sarah, wait." Long fingers curled around her left forearm.

This time she refused to look at him. Mainly, because she needed to concentrate on not reacting to his touch, which was extremely difficult to do when she became trapped in those green eyes. *Sophie's eyes.* "Why would I do that? I have eight missing children to find. This is my first lead. I'm not waiting around for you to decide to share your secrets. Maybe your case is about this Dr. Meltzer and his evil experiments, but mine is about finding those kids before they end up statistics."

"If we don't stop Meltzer, his work will continue. How many more children will he sacrifice to science?"

Like she needed a reminder. "I need the whole truth, Tom."

"I've watched Avalon for three months. Waiting for anything that might give me a legitimate reason to get a warrant and turn that place upside down. My source had me keeping an eye on Dr. Kira Gerard, a Pediatric Geneticist, but she died two weeks ago. With her out of the picture, my investigation stalled. Meltzer hasn't been on staff for years. I had no reason to look at him…until now."

"Your source?" Sarah glared at him. "I thought this morning was the first time you'd met Schneider?"

"He wasn't my first Avalon source." Tom looked away. "Jenny Collins, an RN, contacted me a few months ago. She worked directly with Gerard."

Sarah couldn't respond for several seconds. Finally, she regained enough of her composure to demand, "You're telling me that you've been watching Avalon for three months." She pulled free of his touch. "Two weeks ago this geneticist your source gave up dies and children suddenly start going missing—children you discovered were connected to Avalon. And you did nothing to stop it!"

This was incredible!

"It wasn't until the Myers child went missing that I picked up on the case. His rare illness matched the list of possibilities in the profile of random errors. Even then, it wasn't until the Adams's child was taken that I recognized the connection."

Sarah wrestled in a deep breath. The idea that he had known this and hadn't told her—not even after Cashion's confession—was too much. "I'll ask you again, what're we waiting for? Why not move in for questioning and a search of the doctor's properties? If all you say is true, there's probable cause for a warrant."

"We don't know where the children are. What if he has a backup plan in place? If anything goes wrong, the children might be terminated. We can't stop that from happening if we don't know where they are. It's imperative that we know the children's location before we make a move."

His reasoning made sense, but something was wrong here. "What about Meltzer's cell phone records? Shouldn't we be getting a warrant for those?" Sarah looked around, checked in front of and behind his SUV. "Where's your backup? I haven't seen you make the first call to give updates on what we've discovered. Where's the rest of your team, Tom? Who are you reporting to?"

"Like I said." he stared forward, his face wiped clean of emotion. "There are things I can't share."

He was lying to her. She couldn't believe it. Too stunned to trust herself to say more, Sarah stared at the home across the street. What were they going to do? Sit here all night and watch for the man to make a move? She powered her window down and inhaled the night air. The wind coming off the water was crisp and clean. *Deep breath. Hold it. Release slowly.* She needed to get out and walk. The anxiety was building. Her heart and pulse rate were escalating.

God, she did not want this to happen now.

Tom was already looking for chinks in her armor. She wasn't about to give him exactly what he was looking for. The pill she'd downed before the second interview with Cashion had long since worn off. Unless she climbed out of the SUV and ran a few miles, there might be no way around the unpleasant business of taking another right in front of him. *Think about anything else.*

They were parked in the driveway of a summerhouse. That was Sarah's contribution to their impotent stakeout. She'd called a realtor contact and acquired extensive information on the properties on this prestigious cul-de-sac. Two of the four homes were only occupied from the end of May until mid-September. She'd also learned that Meltzer had purchased his property for three and a half million dollars seven years ago. His wife had passed away five years ago. They had no children. He lived in that enormous house all alone.

Just like you, Sarah. All alone.

Her chest grew tighter. She couldn't keep sitting here. A deep breath was impossible. "I need to take a walk."

Sarah was out of the car before Tom could stop her this time. It was dark. No one was going to notice. A couple of lights had come on inside the

Meltzer house, but there was no landscape lighting to chase away the deepening gloom of dusk.

Mostly, she just needed space. She'd been cramped up in the SUV with Tom most of the day. She couldn't bear to breathe in his scent anymore. She didn't want to hear the sound of his voice. She pressed her fingertips to her eyes and took a breath. All she had to do was get through the next hour or so. Once she was home and away from him, she would be okay. She could call Larson and they would figure out how to proceed.

"Still having the panic attacks?"

Sarah braced herself, swallowed back the hostile response that wanted to lash from her. There was one house on this side of the street as well as the one they were watching that were occupied. Drawing attention to their presence would prove counterproductive.

"Yes." To hell with what he thought. Sarah reached into her bag and dug out her prescription bottle. She opened the bottle with shaking hands and popped the much-needed relief. When she'd swallowed it down, she went on, "Panic attacks. Nightmares. I have to remind myself to eat." She shook the bottle before dropping it into her purse. "This is my life, Tom. Aren't you glad you asked?"

She paced the drive from his SUV to the garage, back and forth. He let her. Didn't say a word, in fact. He went over to the front porch steps and sat down.

If this was her house she would have some sort of motion sensor lights. The yard and drive were completely dark. At this moment, she appreciated the advantage, but who leaves a multi-million dollar property unattended and unprotected like this?

"People with the big bucks," she muttered.

Not that it was any of her business. The security analysis was just a distraction.

She'd been involved with enough stakeouts to know this was the way it worked more often than not. Hours and hours were spent waiting and hoping for any little thing that might move the investigation forward. She just didn't like being on a stakeout with her ex-husband. Not quite ex, she reminded herself.

Stop lying to yourself, Sarah. The real problem was the undeniable fact that she couldn't stop reacting to him on a level that had nothing to do with being a cop. The sound of his voice, the way he looked at her—Jesus Christ, his touch—every part of him awakened feelings she hadn't experienced in years. How on earth could he still do that?

Her errant gaze sought and found him seated on those steps, his attention seemingly focused across the street, his hands hanging between his spread knees. It was too dark to see his face. She could well imagine what was going on in his head. If telling him the truth hurt his feelings or made him judge her, well that was just too bad.

She wanted to find those missing kids. He was standing squarely in the way of the one damned decent lead uncovered in two weeks and even it hinged on Tom's word and that of a suspected killer. Her temper flared again. This was why they shouldn't be working this case together. All she wanted to do was yell at him until he went away. How could she focus on the case with him this close? He…confused her, disabled her defenses.

Livid all over again, she walked past his SUV and to the street that curled around the cul-de-sac. The house right next to Meltzer's was empty for the winter. She'd wanted to burrow in there, but Tom had disagreed. Too close, he'd said.

The streetlamps discreetly placed around the cul-de-sac were gas operated and gave off little illumination. People in high-end neighborhoods like this didn't want the lights obscuring the stars or invading their privacy. That was a good thing under the circumstances. She could walk the cul-de-sac without being spotted unless someone came outside with a flashlight. It was cloudy enough to prevent the moon from being a concern. Her clothes were dark so no worries there. At least she could walk off some of this damned tension.

Had Tom requested a wiretap for the good doctor's phone? Not to her knowledge. They hadn't been apart since the big revelation from Cashion. Tom hadn't called for a warrant. He hadn't done a damned thing, which meant they were wasting precious minutes and hours!

By the time Sarah stopped her mental rant, she was all the way around the loop and passing the end of the Meltzer's driveway. There were other homes on neighboring streets. If spotted, as far as anyone knew she could be a health nut out for late night stroll. This wasn't suspicious at all. *Right.* This was a perfect example of why emotions had no place on the job.

"Sarah."

She whipped around, startled. He'd decided to follow her and she hadn't noticed. Just further evidence that she wasn't up to par in his presence. The concept made her angry—mostly at herself.

"Walking around out here isn't a smart move. It's better if no one knows we're here."

"Yeah, well, I needed some space." She headed back down the drive where his SUV waited. No need to pretend, he knew the ugly truth now.

"Get in the car."

She glanced across the hood at the man who'd spoken. "I need to keep moving." If she kept walking, even if only up and down the driveway, the panic would recede a lot faster.

"We should talk," he said, his tone gentler now.

"What I want to know is why aren't we talking to him?" She gestured toward the house at the end of the long tree-lined drive across the street. "We're wasting time. Maybe I should just call a friend for a ride home." Not that she had any friends, really. She had colleagues and business contacts, but she didn't have any friends. Did Carla count? Maybe. Sarah wasn't sure of anything anymore.

The heavy night air shuddered into her lungs. No Carla didn't count. They weren't friends. They were companions in agony. Agony had brought them together and it kept them apart except on the rare occasions when hope dared to make a fleeting appearance. How could you be friends when all you shared was the kind of unspeakable horror no one wanted to know?

How could you be a wife to a man who knew what you'd done? A man who, when you looked at him, all you could see was the loss and devastation you had caused.

"Trust me, Sarah," Tom pleaded. "Trust me and I swear I'll explain everything. You just have to give me a couple of days."

For one long moment, she could only stare into those eyes that haunted her dreams when she managed to sleep. She steeled herself against those softer emotions. "Trust you? The way I did when you had me committed to that hospital and the little white room that was nothing more than a padded cell." That old anger ignited inside her. "They kept me in that box for thirty-six hours. They kept me drugged for a week." She shook her head. "All because my daughter was missing and I was desperate to find her. All I wanted was my daughter and somehow that was unacceptable."

He looked away.

"That's right," she accused. "That's what you did. You took me there and then you left. Don't ask me to trust you again, Tom, because I won't. *Ever.*"

"You weren't eating or sleeping. You were killing yourself, Sarah. I had to do something before it was too late."

She laughed. "You think you saved me?" She shook her head. "You didn't save me, Tom. The only reason I didn't end it all the minute I got out of that place was because I promised Carla I would be there for her. That's it. My decision had nothing to do with *you*."

He nodded. "Fair enough."

Her words had hit the mark and done some damage. She knew this. Fine. She didn't care. What had he come here expecting?

"Give me forty-eight hours. If I haven't convinced you we're on the right track by then, I'll get out of your way."

Forty-eight hours. Two days. "All right. You have forty-eight hours. What now?"

"Now I'm sending you home to get some sleep and I'm staying here to keep watch."

"What happened to talking?" He wasn't getting the forty-eight hours without an explanation. He'd said they should talk. Now was his chance.

Maybe his last chance.

"I'll tell you everything I can for now. I swear."

CHAPTER EIGHTEEN

"Where is Tom now, Sarah?" Chief Larson asked, his voice reflecting the same concern she saw in his eyes.

Sarah looked from her boss, a man she had known and trusted for twelve years, to the stranger he had introduced as Special Agent Jerry Swinwood, and back. A deeply ingrained need to protect the man with whom she had once shared everything kicked in. "I have no idea. What's this about?"

Tom had called a taxi to take her home shortly after two this morning. He'd urged Sarah to get some sleep before they met later today. He hadn't said where they would meet or if he planned to get any sleep. He'd just said they would rendezvous later.

Her cell had awakened her at half past eight. She'd overslept by more than an hour. Chief Larson hadn't sounded happy when he called wanting her in his office ASAP. A shower and two cups of coffee later she'd driven straight here. Every phone in the building seemed to be ringing as she'd rushed past cubicles and offices. Before she'd had a minute to scan the messages on her desk Larson had ushered her into this closed door meeting with Swinwood. So far, she'd answered their questions truthfully, until the last one. Technically, Tom could be anywhere so she hadn't exactly lied.

"Detective," Swinwood said, taking his turn, "can you tell me what you and Agent Cuddahy have been doing for the past forty-eight hours?"

Sarah didn't like him. In all her years at Metro she'd never had trouble working with the FBI or any of the other three letter agencies. There was something about the way this agent looked at her and said Tom's name that bugged her.

"We have eight missing children, Agent Swinwood," Sarah pointed out. "Agent Cuddahy is assisting with interviews of the victims' parents. I'm sure Chief Larson filled you in."

Over the weekend, the media had dubbed the investigation the *Negligent Nanny case*. As Sarah had feared, the abduction of the senator's daughter had sent the media into a frenzy. The community was afraid for their children, as they well should be. They wanted more information than given by the shocking reports meant for selling newspapers and upping Nielsen ratings. So they called. Those who weren't afraid, wanted to help. A few were simply loons with nothing better to do than to use up valuable time and resources.

"You interviewed Lawrence Cashion again yesterday," Agent Swinwood went on as if she'd explained nothing. "What did you and Agent Cuddahy learn from him?"

"Detective Cuddahy always files her reports promptly," Larson interjected. "With the long hours she's been working to find these children the paperwork is a little behind." He looked directly at Sarah then. "I trust she'll bring me up to speed in a timely manner."

Larson was warning her. He was worried. Swinwood and his questions were trouble.

"I appreciate that, sir." She shifted her attention to the fed. "We didn't learn anything beneficial to the investigation. Mr. Cashion has no memory of the timeframe when his daughter and wife went missing. I'm confident you've read the report he gave the first officers on the scene after his wife and daughter went missing. He's terrified that he killed his wife, but he has no recall of the event."

"He told you nothing else?"

"No one wants to find these children more than I do, Agent Swinwood." Her patience was at an end. "If Cashion had provided useful information I would be following up on that information and sharing it with the Joint Task Force. Maybe you'd feel more comfortable interviewing him personally."

"That would be optimal, Detective, except Lawrence Cashion is dead."

Sarah looked to Larson. "When did this happen? Why wasn't I informed?" She and Tom hadn't left his room until well after three the previous afternoon. He'd been emotional, but he'd seemed stable otherwise.

"He had another heart attack." The guilt in Larson's eyes told her the decision to hold back this information hadn't been his own. "He didn't make it through this one."

She had a bad feeling this meeting was about to take a turn for the worse. "Am I still on this case or what? Because if I am, I need to know—"

"You are not, Detective," Swinwood announced.

Larson dragged a hand over his face.

"What's going on here, Chief?" She had been on this case since the beginning.

"Sarah—"

"If you know where Agent Cuddahy is," Swinwood advised, cutting off Larson, "I suggest you tell me now. This situation—"

"Agent Swinwood," Larson stood, his face darkening with his own mounting anger. Like Sarah, he'd had enough, "I'd like a few minutes with my detective. Alone."

"You understand—" Swinwood began.

"I understand perfectly," Larson confirmed.

Silence thickened in the room until the door had closed behind the agent. "What the hell is going on?" Sarah's throat had gone so dry she couldn't swallow. If she'd been smart she would have had a pill with that second cup of coffee this morning. Too late now. Her pulse was racing. The pounding in her chest was escalating. "Why is this man demanding to know where Tom is?"

Maybe she should have told him, but that would have given away the one lead they had acquired from Cashion. She simply wasn't willing to take the risk until she had a better grasp of the situation. Tom had warned her not to tell anyone. Wasn't the goal of all parties involved to find those children? As much as she wanted to believe that her instincts warned that something was way off. None of this made sense. Bottom line, whether they were still a couple or not, her gut instinct was to protect Tom.

"I don't know whether or not you're aware of Tom's location and I don't have a clue what he's told you, but he's in serious trouble, Sarah. Very serious trouble." Her boss heaved a big breath.

"Tom?" He was the one who always did everything by the book. He never broke the rules. "Are you kidding me?"

Larson shook his head, his expression grim. "Last week an OPR investigation into Tom's activities over the past month was initiated."

There had to be a mistake. Tom was the epitome of an ethical man and agent. The Office of Professional Responsibility couldn't be investigating him. The idea was absurd.

"There has to be some mistake."

"A woman died, Sarah. A Dr. Kira Gerard. This Swinwood character believes Tom is somehow responsible for her death."

Panic slithered along Sarah's spine. "That's impossible and you know it."

Larson turned up his hands. "The Tom I used to know was above reproach. Is he still that same man?" Before Sarah could answer, Larson added, "Tragedy changes people, Sarah. You know that better than anyone. He lost his little girl and then he lost you. Maybe he lost a lot more that we don't know about."

For a moment she was at a loss for words. For five long years people had looked at her that way. *Poor Sarah, she lost her daughter, you know. Sad Sarah, she'll never be the same. Never be whole.* This was Tom they were talking about. The rock. He had weathered the storm and come through it standing tall and strong and still reaching his hand out to her. Was she missing something? Had he fallen apart inside where no one could see? Wouldn't she notice the change? She knew every part of him by heart. Had she been so successful in closing him out and blocking the memories that she failed to recognize that level of change?

No way.

Indignation plowed through Sarah, clearing away the uncertainty. "We both lost...more than anyone knows. As awful as that reality is, Tom is still the same good man he was before. I can vouch for him."

Another troubled sigh escaped Larson. "That makes what I have to do all the more difficult."

Sarah braced and wished to hell a truckload of emotion weren't parked on her chest. "What're you talking about?"

"Swinwood didn't start with me, Sarah. Word came down the chain of command from the Chief of Police's office. Senator Adams is not happy and he's fanning the flames. He started making calls yesterday. I spoke to a friend at the local field office and he says whatever is going on with Tom has gone from an internal FBI investigation to a full-fledged witch-hunt. That same unpleasantness has spilled over to you. I was ordered to take you off this case."

A combination of ire and fear churned inside her. "I've been the lead detective representing Metro in this investigation from the beginning. I know the children, the parents, and everyone else involved better than anyone." How could she help these children if she was off the case?

"There's nothing I can do." Larson schooled the sympathy from his face, but not before she got a good look. He knew this was wrong. "Turn over everything you have to Sergeant Riggs. We have to do this right, Sarah. Chief Timmons will have my head if I don't see that this gets done."

Larson was three years away from retirement. As angry as Sarah was she didn't want to cause him any grief for a decision that was not his own.

"All right." She stood. "If I'm off the case I guess I'll take some of that leave time I have accumulated."

"As much as I need you around here, that's a good idea. You haven't taken a vacation in—"

"Eighteen months," she said before he could. And that hadn't exactly been a vacation. "Anything else I need to know or do before I go?"

"Stay away from Tom," Larson advised. "I understand he's still your husband, but I don't want you dragged into whatever is going on with him."

"Easy enough," she lied. She stood, prepared to go. The sooner she turned her files over to Riggs, the sooner she could get out of here and demand some answers from Tom.

"Be careful, Sarah," Larson cautioned. "I know you too well to believe you'll take a vacation with those kids missing. Whatever you do, just make sure it's not something we'll both regret."

"Wouldn't dream of it."

Sarah went straight to her desk. She had nothing else to say to Swinwood. If he wanted to ask more questions he could ask Larson. She was officially on vacation.

She might be off the Task Force and the case, but they couldn't stop her from doing all within her power to find those children on her own.

2569 Edge Cove Road
St. Michaels, Maryland, 4:05 p.m.

"For the third time, no one followed me."

Tom sensed a new kind of tension in Sarah. Considering what he was asking her to do the reaction was understandable. "Where'd you park your car?"

"Two streets over." Her attention lingered across the street, on Meltzer's house. "Have you been here all day?"

Worry worked its way through Tom now. Something was wrong. "I'm not leaving until he does."

"I figured that would be your answer." She shifted the tote bag from her shoulder and passed it to him. "I brought sandwiches and drinks. Chips, peanuts, cookies."

Still not looking at him, she moved back to the large window at the front of the great room. Her hands were braced on her hips. Oh yeah. She had something more than the case on her mind.

"Thanks." He'd eaten the last pack of snack crackers he could find in his SUV hours ago. Once he'd gotten the key to the house, he'd scoured the pantry and popped some ramen noodles into the microwave. The place was fully furnished with a partially stocked pantry. He'd called the leasing agent first thing this morning. She'd brought the key to him before noon.

He was here for the duration.

As long as Sarah hadn't already given him up.

He should have told her the truth already. The trouble was the truth was complicated. The last thing he'd wanted to do was to involve her. How had she ended up on this case? This kind of pressure couldn't be doing her any favors.

"I take it you leased the house since I didn't see any indication of breaking and entering." She turned to face him now, her face clean of emotion.

"I did."

She nodded. "You used an alias, I assume."

"Of course."

Her attention settled on the sofa table he'd covered with electronic equipment. "This is why you're not glued to the window with a pair of binoculars?"

They'd spent the better part of last night monitoring the house across the street from the front seat of his SUV or the porch with binoculars.

"I'm listening as well as watching." He indicated the monitor. "If the garage door opens or a vehicle pulls into or out of the driveway, I'll know it. I pick up the occasional snippet of conversation and a television somewhere in the house on a news channel."

Ten or so seconds elapsed with her studying the equipment. "How far were you planning to go with this before you told me the truth?"

She had at least part of the story it seemed. "I was going to tell you."

"At what point? When you were arrested? When my career was placed in jeopardy because you couldn't trust me with the whole story?"

"That's not the way it is."

"Then explain to me how it is, Tom, because the agent waiting for me at my office had some pretty damning things to say about you."

Tom's heart rate kicked up. "Swinwood?" Bastard. "Did you tell him about Meltzer?"

"Yes. Agent Swinwood. He wanted to know what Cashion said, I told him he couldn't remember what happened to his wife and child. That's *all* I told him."

Tom dared to take a deep breath. "What about Larson?"

"I told him the same thing." She walked closer, searched his eyes. "That was right before he took me off the case."

"Oh hell, Sarah. I didn't mean for this to happen." Damn. He set the bag of food down and hoped he could find the right words to explain. "I told you I'd been watching Avalon. I couldn't pinpoint the connection at first, but then I found a weak link in the chain. A way to get inside information, at least I hoped I'd be able to."

"Dr. Gerard."

Tom shouldn't be surprised that Sarah had been briefed, yet somehow he was. "I watched Gerard for a month. I dug until I found what I needed and then I used it to pressure her into meeting with me."

The disappointment in Sarah's eyes hurt him far more than the idea of losing his job. When had he become that man? The one who would do anything to get the results he wanted?

"Did she agree to help?"

"She agreed to talk to me. We had several conversations before she was ready to share what she originally denied knowing. I was to follow her to the location of her choosing. She was terrified of being caught talking to me." Images and sounds from that night flickered through his mind. "Only she didn't make it. They claimed she was driving too fast and missed the curve, but I was behind her and she wasn't driving too fast. She never hit the brakes or tried to avoid going into the ravine."

"What do you think happened?"

"I think she was drugged when she drove off the road."

"Was someone else in the car with her?"

"She was alone. She started weaving a little. I thought she was trying to use her phone." God he was so tired. But he couldn't stop. Not until this was done. "Then she drove over the edge. I can only assume she ingested the drug before she got in the car to drive to our rendezvous location."

"There was no autopsy?"

"Oh, yeah, there was an autopsy. According to the autopsy report the tox screen was clean. The Avalon administrator claimed she made a phone call to him saying I was following her and that she feared for her safety. Two weeks later I was put on administrative leave pending the OPR investigation."

"If she was drugged and the tox screen was falsified, then you've made yourself a powerful enemy. Not just anyone could make that happen."

"Tell me something I don't know."

"Cashion is dead."

"How?"

"Another heart attack. Late last night."

"And Meltzer didn't come home until almost midnight." Tom moved to the window and stared across the street at the house where Meltzer was holed up. He was the one. Tom felt it deep in his gut. When he'd pushed Gerard, she wouldn't say. Then, that last time they'd talked, something in her voice had told him she'd changed her mind about telling him what she knew, but she hadn't gotten the chance.

"Meltzer found out Cashion talked," Sarah suggested.

"They're in cleanup mode." Tom had recognized the pattern as soon as the fourth child went missing. The same maneuver had been attempted in Paradise. Meltzer understood he was caught. If Tom didn't watch him closely he would disappear and set up someplace else under a new identity.

Three evil brothers had walked away from those Nazi concentration camps all those years ago. They assumed new identities and eventually settled in the United States. Two of the brothers were long dead, their sadistic heirs either deceased or in prison. Only one brother remained unaccounted for. If Tom was right, since Meltzer was too young to be the missing brother, he was the son. According to the research Sarah had done, Meltzer's father was dead, which meant the last of the three devils who'd migrated here after the war was in hell where he belonged.

All Tom had to do now was stop his son.

Whatever the cost, Tom had to catch Meltzer before he disappeared. Those children had to be rescued…and any others out there they didn't know about yet. He didn't have the element of surprise on his side this time as he had in Paradise. Meltzer knew Tom was close.

"So, what do we do to stop him and to find those kids?"

"First," Tom looked deep into those worried brown eyes, prayed he could do this without causing her further pain, "we don't get caught."

"And after that?"

"We don't give up."

CHAPTER NINETEEN

"Sarah."

Sarah jerked awake. "What?" She hadn't meant to fall asleep.

"We have to go. Meltzer's on the move."

She grabbed her bag as she shoved her feet into her shoes. "I'm ready." On second thought, she reached for the bag with the snacks. "Let's go."

If Meltzer left the house, Tom wanted to follow him. Sarah ignored the voice of uncertainty. Agent Swinwood had to be wrong about Tom. If a man as strong as Tom could fall apart there was no hope for anyone else.

Once they were loaded into his SUV he turned on one of his gadgets and handed it to her. "You keep an eye on that and I'll keep mine on the road."

Sarah stared at the electronic device for a moment. It looked like a typical GPS you might use for getting from point A to point B, but this wasn't giving them directions—the screen was tracking the movements of Meltzer's car.

"When did you have the opportunity to put a tracking device on his vehicle?"

"The less you know about what I did while you were gone today the better. Just be glad I was able to do it. We can't afford to get too close. If he realizes we're following him we won't be finding those children."

The cold that seeped into Sarah's bones held her silent for a long while. There was no way to see this as anything other than what it was. Tom had broken the law—more than once she feared. Yes, the circumstances warranted decisive action. She would be the first person to admit as much. Still, Tom had to know this kind of move could get any evidence they discovered thrown out. Unless he had a warrant in his pocket what they were doing was as illegal as hell. The certainty she'd felt last night had waned a bit.

"It's a risk," he confessed, as if he'd heard her thoughts.

Sarah studied his profile in the dim glow from the dash lights. She wished she could see his eyes— the eyes she didn't like looking at. "A big one."

"This is our only option, Sarah. You surely see the dilemma we're facing. If there's any chance of saving those kids, we have to act fast. This is the only way."

"That's usually my line." Chief Larson had lectured her plenty of times about skirting the fringes of the law. She just hadn't expected to ever need to give that lecture to Tom.

"If he gets away the likelihood of finding him is negligible at best."

"We can't let that happen," she agreed.

"However this plays out," he glanced at her through the darkness, "I'm in charge. I gave the orders. You're operating under the impression that I have the necessary paper to back up my actions."

"Except Agent Swinwood has already warned me that's not the case."

She shouldn't have had to remind him of that point. He really was off his game. For one thing, he needed sleep. Was that all he needed? Tom had never so much as taken an aspirin when he had a headache. He was the last person on earth who would abuse drugs, even prescription ones. Had he started drinking? She hadn't picked up on any signs of alcohol abuse. She'd never seen him drink more than a beer or two, not even after it became clear they wouldn't be finding their daughter. However angry she remained at him for what he'd done eighteen months ago, on this case she was with him one hundred percent. Finding those children was all that mattered.

"You've got me there. I guess we'll just have to cross that bridge when we come to it—after Meltzer is in custody."

"While we're on the subject," she checked the tracking device, "why don't you tell me a little more about that bridge?"

"There's nothing to tell. I was set up. The goal was to get me off this investigation. Someone doesn't want me to finish this. I'm this close." He held his forefinger and thumb barely a half-inch apart. "I'm not walking away now."

"You said your investigation started in Tennessee with Paul Phillips." It was difficult for Sarah to talk about the man without thinking of his inability to help her find Sophie. She'd been desperate enough to ask for his help. She gave her head a little shake. That level of desperation does things to a person. "That was more than a year ago, did the investigation go cold or was it shut down?"

Tom didn't answer for a long moment and she knew she'd guessed correctly.

"At first I had the full backing of the Bureau. They wanted to find the third brother and to stop him as well as undo as much of the harm he'd created as humanly possible." He laughed. The sound held no humor. "I think maybe undo was always the wrong goal. Stopping him, if by chance he's still alive, and his son, as well as any other followers is the goal I have now. You can't undo the kinds of things these bastards do, but maybe we can stop this from happening again."

She'd suspected his objective was different from hers. "Finding the children alive would be nothing more than a perk to you. Meltzer is the primary objective."

He didn't speak for a moment and his silence was answer enough.

"They shut down the investigation, Sarah. They shut it down and declared the work a waste of resources. You know what that means as well as I do—Meltzer has someone in his pocket high enough up the food chain to make that kind of decision. This man—this madman—has to be stopped. If I don't finish this, no one will."

He paused for a moment, his tension palpable. "Yes, I want to find those children alive, but I won't lie to you by saying my top priority is anything other than catching Meltzer. He could have dozens of doctors out there playing God. There could be hundreds of cloned and designer children like the ones you're looking for that we don't know about."

"*If* Meltzer is the one."

"He's the one."

"You're willing to stake your career—fifteen-years of distinguished service—on that?"

"Whatever it takes," he reminded her. "I saw what they did to Paul and the people in Paradise. The genetic tampering you've read or heard about is nothing compared to the damage these people have done. Someone has to be willing to take the necessary risks to stop it."

"So we just keep following him?" Sarah studied the GPS as Meltzer's vehicle closed in on Highway 50.

"That's the plan."

"What if we're wrong?" Worry gnawed at her. "What if we're chasing a dead end?"

"Larson took you off the case," he reminded her. "Without a lead you were at a dead end anyway. This is the only lead we have."

She didn't like his reasoning, but she couldn't argue the accuracy of it. There were no leads, no evidence, and with her officially off the investigation, she wouldn't be privy to anything new the Task Force learned. Her gaze sought Tom in the near darkness. At the moment his theory was the only option she had.

Tom was one of the smartest men she knew. He was damned good at his work and he loved being a federal agent. If he was willing to risk his career, that meant this case was as important to him as it was to Sarah, perhaps for different reasons, but the determination to see it through was there. She had nothing to lose by sticking with him and his potential lead.

Why not see where it led?

7:30 A.M.

Sarah felt the car slow and she opened her eyes. She peered out at the passing landscape. Nothing but trees. The fall colors were a somber reminder that Christmas was only two months away. *Another holiday without Sophie.*

Blinking away the thought Sarah glanced at the time on the dash. They'd been on the road for almost five hours. "Where are we?"

"We passed through Williamsport about fifteen minutes ago."

"Pennsylvania?"

"That's the one." He glanced at the GPS. "Looks like he's slowing for a turn. I'm hoping that means he's nearing his destination."

Another three or four minutes passed before the red dot that represented Meltzer's vehicle stopped moving. Sarah's pulse reacted to a surge of adrenaline. "He could be refueling."

"He stopped for gas an hour ago."

"This could be it."

"Let's hope so."

Sarah studied his profile. His beard-shadowed jaw made her think of all those mornings she'd awakened next to him. The feel of his hands on her skin and his lips against her ear ricocheted through her heart. Every morning of their life together he had whispered the same greeting in her ear, "*good morning, you are my favorite part of waking up.*"

The memories made her sad. Sarah turned away from him and stared out the window. That life was over. Even as the words formed in her mind, her heart dared to believe otherwise. *Don't go there.*

Shifting her attention to the road the wooded landscape gave way to a hole-in-the-wall town called Willow Creek. Shops, most vacant, dotted the main street. Sarah noted a market, gas station, post office, and small City Hall, all practically next door to each other. As they left the four blocks that represented the downtown area behind, modest homes took the place of the shops on either side of the street.

Tom made the right turn Meltzer had taken minutes ago. The paved road cut through the woods. There was an old house or two, then nothing except trees. Occasionally Sarah glimpsed a boarded up house or chimney standing alone deep amid the trees.

Easing to the side of the road, Tom shifted into park. "Let's have a look at what's up ahead."

Sarah passed the GPS monitor to him. With a few taps of the screen Tom had opened Google Earth and was scanning a bird's eye view of the area. From the shops back in town to the ramshackle structures hidden in the woods their location appeared on the screen as if they'd just flown a drone over the area.

A long, low whistle blew past Tom's lips. He zoomed in on the spot where Meltzer's vehicle had ended its journey. "Looks like a compound of some sort."

Sarah did a little googling on her smart phone. "It's an old tuberculosis sanatorium. It's been abandoned for half a century."

"We need a closer look."

Tom turned his SUV around, which took some doing considering how narrow the road was.

"We passed a couple of abandoned houses." He scanned the trees on either side of the road. "Let's find the closest one."

Sarah leaned forward. "There. On the right." She pointed to a gravel drive—or what had once been a gravel drive—that was grown over with weeds for the most part. "Maybe this one will be in better shape than the others between here and town."

Tom pointed the nose of his SUV into the tangle of low hanging limbs and waist high grass. The scrub of wood against metal made Sarah grimace. "You may need a new paint job after this."

"As long as the engine keeps running and the tires don't go flat, we're good."

Sarah hadn't thought of the potential for running over something that would puncture one or more tires. Getting stuck out here with no transportation would be a nightmare. Not to mention it would put the brakes on their unofficial investigation. And maybe their lives.

The realization that they were in dicey territory and she hadn't felt the first trickle of panic startled her. She hadn't taken a pill since…night before last and she'd slept like the dead last night. As a matter of fact, she hadn't even thought about a panic attack much less worried about having one until just this moment. She glanced at Tom again. She doubted it had anything to do with him. His presence—the mere sound of his voice when he called—usually had the opposite effect.

Stop the overanalyzing and just be grateful.

The house they discovered beyond the trees was still standing. From the road the chimney on each end and part of the roof were all she'd been able to see. Part of the metal that had once covered the roof was long gone. The old board and batten siding had more than a few holes. The local wildlife had likely claimed the place ages ago.

Tom shut off the engine. "You ready for a walk in the woods?"

Sarah surveyed the thick underbrush. "Let's just hope the snakes have gone into hibernation." It was definitely cold enough. She shivered. When she'd tugged on her coat she joined Tom at the front of his SUV. He passed her a pair of the binoculars.

"Stay behind me," he ordered as he headed into the trees.

"Gladly." She had no desire to be the first to forge through this jungle-like terrain.

The underbrush tore at her clothes. Sarah didn't want to think what might be hidden in those bushes. She hadn't spent much time in the country, much less the woods, as a kid. This was a first.

Rather than fret about what might rush out of the bushes to attack her at any moment, she fixated on Tom's broad shoulders. She doubted he'd had any sleep before they hit the road. She could use some coffee about now. She wondered if Tom had eaten. She hadn't eaten, but that wasn't unusual. Food held no appeal for her anymore. She forced herself to eat out of necessity.

She wondered if Tom kept any secrets. He said there was no one else. She wasn't sure she believed him. He was a handsome man. She couldn't imagine he hadn't received plenty of offers. They hadn't shared a bed in more than a year. What man as young, fit, and handsome as Tom ignored his physical needs for that long?

Or, maybe he was like Sarah and had no needs. She hadn't yearned for anything other than work in what felt like forever. It was true that sometimes she dreamed of seeing Sophie and making love with Tom. The dreams were always memories from before…

Tom stopped abruptly. She bumped into his back.

She would have apologized, but he looked back at her, a finger to his lips.

Maybe fifteen yards ahead of their position was an iron fence. Tom dropped into a crouch. Sarah did the same. She lifted her binoculars and surveyed the array of buildings beyond the fence. The old three-story stone structure that had once been a sanatorium had undergone a fairly recent facelift. New windows and state of the art doors ensured tight security. Another, newer building had been added on the west end of the main building. Uniformed guards patrolled the perimeter of both buildings.

No vehicles were visible, which suggested there was a parking area or garage somewhere on the other side of the buildings. The fence was twelve or so feet high and appeared to encompass the property, separating it from the forest. Many of the trees had lost their leaves already, but most sported deep hues of orange and russet, a vivid contrast to the somber gray limestone of the old sanatorium and the steel gray of the new structure.

It was so quiet.

Sarah lowered her binoculars. The occasional call of a bird and the whisper of the wind were the only sounds.

Tom touched her arm. She leaned closer to him.

"Check the second window from the east end on the third floor."

Sarah lifted her binoculars once more and zoomed in on the window. "What? I don't see anything."

He leaned close again. "It was a little blond girl. Maybe the Adams child."

Heart pounding now, Sarah looked again. She checked every window and found nothing. "Are you sure?"

"This is the place, Sarah. I can feel it. Those kids are in there."

CHAPTER TWENTY

2:00 P.M.

They'd watched the compound for hours before settling on a game plan. Sarah's legs ached from crouching for so long. She hadn't seen the little blond girl or any other child.

He lost his little girl and then he lost you. Maybe he lost a lot more that we don't know about.

What if Chief Larson was right? She glanced at the man behind the wheel as he parked in front of what appeared to be an old-fashioned general store. He looked the same other than the glimpses of desolation she saw in his eyes. *Sophie's eyes.*

He was a little leaner, yes, and time and pain had carved a few more lines, otherwise he had scarcely changed. He sounded the same. Smelled the same. The idea of whether he tasted the same came as a surprise. She closed her eyes and shook her head. That path would only lead to trouble she didn't need.

"You okay?"

Sarah started at the question. "Yes. I'm…fine. I was just thinking."

"You're worried that I'm delusional or, worse, that I'm lying to you to keep you cooperative. I know what I saw, Sarah. There was a child. Female. Blond."

His tone was openly defensive. It was one she used far too often. "I believe you, Tom. Why don't we call Larson or Captain Andrews, the Task Force commander? If Katie Adams is at that compound the other children may be as well. We could find out now, today, rather than waiting around to see what happens next."

They'd had this conversation a couple hours ago. Actually, what they'd had was a shouting match inside the old dilapidated house. It was a miracle the thing hadn't fallen in on them.

"We have to be certain." He looked straight ahead now. "If we tip our hand too quickly we could be making a mistake."

His reasoning made no more sense now than it had two hours ago. "If even one of the children is in there, how can a rescue be a mistake?"

Unless he wasn't so sure about what he'd seen. She hated herself for thinking about Tom that way. As much as she still resented what he'd done when he'd committed her to that damned clinic, she'd never lost her respect for him or his ability as an investigator.

The uncertainty plaguing her felt like a betrayal. Maybe because the idea of others questioning her ability was so damned painful. She knew how it felt to have her every move scrutinized. The last thing she wanted was to make him feel that sharp criticism of his work, too.

"Let's do what we came here to do so we can get back to our post."

He was out of the SUV before she could respond. She climbed out as well. At the store's entrance she put her hand on his arm. The shock of touching him made her flinch. "When we get back, I'll take the first watch. You're getting some sleep."

Anger tightened the grim features of his face. "I'm fine, Sarah."

How many times had she said that at a moment like this? "No one is fine without sleep, Tom. No arguments. We have to be able to count on each other. I can't count on you if you're running on empty. Are we clear?"

He heaved a heavy breath. "We are."

He didn't meet her gaze as he ground out the words, but she felt confident she'd made her point.

Inside, the smell of logs on the fire permeated the country atmosphere of the store. The crackling sound reminded her just how cold it was outside. The wood and beamed ceilings brought to mind images of grand old barns. The store was larger than it looked. The old wood floors creaked here and there as Sarah moved down the toiletries aisle. Tom had chosen a different aisle. Suited Sarah. A few minutes away from him would hopefully help give her some perspective.

As she'd gathered the store was a multi-purpose one with a bit of everything. She needed a few personal items. A toothbrush and toothpaste as well as deodorant. She picked up some for Tom as well. Spotting ladies' underwear, she breathed a sigh of relief. They were the plain white cotton brief style, but that worked. She grabbed a three-pack in her size. Maybe some lotion, hand sanitizer, and toilet paper. Using the woods for taking care of business was, unfortunately, the only option for the duration. On second thought, she also grabbed a package of pre-moistened towelettes. Without running water, this was as good as it was going to get where bathing was concerned.

The prospect that both she and Tom had lost their minds was feeling more and more like a viable possibility. Then again, she reminded herself that some people went to a lot of trouble for a rustic vacation getaway in the woods.

By the time she made her way to the counter, Tom was already paying for his purchases. Extra bottled water, ready-to-eat food, and a battery operated lantern with additional batteries. Sarah refused his offer to pay for her items. He held the door for her as they exited.

"I need to find a change of clothes." She scanned the available options lining the block. A second-hand shop appeared to be the only one.

Tom loaded their purchases into the backseat of his SUV. "Hang on and I'll go with you."

"Keep an eye on the GPS. I'll only be a minute." She didn't need him tagging along while she searched for jeans and sweaters.

"Don't take too long," he reminded her. "I'll be right here."

Watching, he didn't have to add. Was he really afraid she would take off on him or that she'd called Larson? She flashed him a smile and crossed the street to the second-hand shop. Pushing open the door set the bells overhead to jangling.

"Afternoon. Welcome to Mia's."

The woman who greeted Sarah looked to be in her late twenties. Untamed red hair and a porcelain complexion. Her vivid blue eyes lit up when she smiled. She reminded Sarah of the women she'd seen in vintage flower child posters from the 60's and 70's her mother had kept. From the headband and the big peace symbol on the necklace she wore to the tattered bellbottoms the shopkeeper was getting in touch with her inner hippie.

"Nice place." Sarah produced a smile for the young woman as she perused the rack of jeans.

"You look like a size two." The young lady parted the jeans at the other end of the rack and motioned for Sarah to join her. "I'm Mia, by the way."

"Sarah." She picked through the size two's.

"At Mia's we believe in reusing and repurposing. Waste is such an ugly thing." She smiled. "New is immensely overrated and way too expensive."

"New is definitely overrated." Sarah's lips stretched into the real McCoy this time. "Have you lived in Willow Creek long?"

Mia shrugged. "Only my whole life."

Sarah selected two pairs of jeans. "These will work."

"You can wear these right away." Mia took the jeans from her. "I don't sell anything I haven't washed. Everything here is ready to wear."

That was definitely good to hear. "Sweaters? Sweatshirts?" Something that would keep her warm and comfortable.

Mia laid the jeans on the counter. "Over here."

Sarah followed her to another rack. After a few moments of watching Mia shuffle hangers, Sarah asked, "What's the deal with the compound just outside town? Looks like a prison or something with that iron fence all around it."

Mia laid several selections across the top of the rack for Sarah's consideration. "When I was a kid we used to sneak over there and go through the rooms of the old sanatorium. It's haunted, you know." She gave Sarah a knowing nod. "They say some of the people who died there just won't leave."

"What kind of sanatorium was it?" The question was a way to prod the woman to talk while Sarah tested the fabric and considered the thickness of the second hand sweaters.

"One of those old tuberculosis sanatoriums." Mia leaned closer as if she feared someone might overhear her. "My grandmother told me they kept crazy people there, too. They performed all sorts of experiments on them. Lots of people went in, only a few came out. She swore there was a secret cemetery around there somewhere, but I never found it."

"What happened to the ones who never left the sanatorium?" Sarah rounded her eyes in order to look properly horrified.

"The official word was that they cremated the bodies to prevent the spread of disease, but my grandmother insisted that was a lie. She thinks they did something terrible to those people. You know, Frankenstein experiments, and then buried them."

"Wouldn't the police have stopped them if that were true?"

Mia laughed. "Are you kidding? That old place kept this town alive back in the day. It was the only source of work for most of the folks around here who weren't farmers. No one was going to rat them out. Not that it would have mattered. The cops were on the payroll as the story goes." She sighed. "I guess every town has its skeletons."

"And legends." Sarah selected three of the sweaters. "What's in the old sanatorium now?"

"Word is it's some kind of medical research place, but if it is no one around here works there." Mia shrugged. "Who knows? It's all hush-hush. Even the cops don't seem to know what's going on behind that ominous gate."

"How strange." Sarah frowned. "A little creepy even. Could be terrorists." She made her eyes go wide again.

"Nah." Mia took the sweaters from her. "It's the same family who owned it back when it was a sanatorium. My grandmother said the son runs the place now."

"Sounds like your grandmother knows a lot of the town's history. I'd love to speak with her."

Mia's face fell. "She died last spring."

"I'm sorry." Sarah followed her to the counter. "I lost my parents and my grandparents before I finished college."

"That had to be tough." Mia folded Sarah's purchases. "I still have my momma, but she moved to Pittsburg with her second husband three years ago. It's just me and my little girl now."

Sarah's chest tightened. "How old is your little girl?"

"She's four." Mia grinned and turned a framed photo toward Sarah. "She's my world."

"She's beautiful." The child was a miniature version of her mother.

"You just passing through?" Mia hit the total on her vintage cash register.

"I'm doing a book on the history of Pennsylvania. I'm traveling all over the state."

"Sounds interesting." Mia took the cash Sarah offered.

"Is there another way into the sanatorium besides that one gate?" Sarah dared to ask. At Mia's look of suspicion, she added, "I haven't found another road to the property. I was just curious."

"The gate and that one road is the only way in or out." She shrugged. "Nothing else but woods."

Sarah smiled. "Thanks. I appreciate the info."

"Fair warning."

Sarah met the other woman's intent gaze.

"They don't like folks poking around at the old sanatorium." Mia bagged Sarah's purchases. "My momma used to yell at me for going over there after they started the remodel. She said it was dangerous and the man who inherited the place was as evil as the devil himself. She said he might do anything. His family was real Nazis, you know." Mia glanced around as if just saying the words out loud made her nervous. "That was a long time ago, but she was so insistent that I haven't ever forgotten her warning."

"You've been far more helpful than you know."

Sarah couldn't wait to tell Tom.

Maybe his wild story about what happened in Paradise, Tennessee, and the brothers who escaped post war Germany wasn't so farfetched after all.

8:00 P.M.

Sarah couldn't sit down if her life depended on it. She'd told Tom what the shop owner had said and he'd acted as if the news was irrelevant. The town gossip more or less confirmed his suspicions about the sanatorium. Why wasn't he glad to hear it?

Keeping her temper in check, she braced her arms over her chest and stared out the dirty broken window. It was dark outside so she couldn't see a damned thing, but beyond those trees, inside that compound, something was going on.

Meltzer was there, no question. Tom had set up a motion sensor near the gate—as near as he'd dared to go anyway. According to Mia, there was no other way in or out.

If someone left the compound, she and Tom would know it.

He'd refused to sleep when they'd returned to the house. Instead, they had spent the hours before dark becoming familiar with the tree line along the fence. They had walked all the way around the compound without seeing a damned thing useful to the investigation. Then he'd organized the part of the house they would use. Sarah had spent that time pacing. For once it had nothing to do with walking off a panic attack. She wanted to do something besides prepare. She wanted to go back out there and watch until something happened.

No. What she really wanted to do was get past that gate.

She looked around what had once been a bedroom in the old house. It was the only room where the roof and floor seemed stable. He'd set up the water and food supply on an abandoned dresser. Then he'd dragged an old bench from another room and stacked his surveillance equipment there. He'd even rounded up a couple of chairs and a small table with one bad leg. The legs of the chairs were uneven and there were holes in the seats, but they worked.

As much as she appreciated his efforts at making the place more comfortable her frustration mounted. He had totally blown off the news from the shopkeeper. He ignored her warnings that he needed sleep. He'd rounded up the sleeping bag from his SUV and spread it on the cleanest spot on the floor, but that was the only time he'd gone near it.

Thankfully, he kept extra blankets in his SUV because it was as cold as hell. Sarah shivered and started walking again. Maybe if she kept moving she would walk off some of her irritation with him. She checked her cell. Service wasn't nonexistent out here, but it was sketchy at best. The urge to call Larson nudged her again.

What was waiting accomplishing?

"Calling in backup at this point would be pointless."

The sound of Tom's voice in the dimly lit space had goose bumps tumbling over her skin. How could he still read her so well after all this time? "You argued that point already."

"But you don't agree."

She turned to glare at him. "Does what I think matter at all? You should be sleeping right now. Then later, I could sleep. You won't be able to do a damned thing when the time comes if you're completely exhausted."

He stopped tinkering with one of the pieces of equipment and moved closer to her. More of those goose bumps raised on her skin. It wasn't fair that he still possessed the power to make her heart pound with nothing more than a look or a move.

"I'll sleep when I need to sleep."

"So you're super human now? You don't require sleep to function?" How was that rational? Sarah recognized the futility of debating him. He wouldn't change his mind any more than she had when he'd insisted she wasn't sleeping or eating. How could he not see he was doing the same thing? Even she recognized it and denial was her middle name.

How could they possibly hope to do this on their own?

"I'm not talking to you about this anymore, Sarah."

She'd heard that before. "The way you stopped talking to me about Sophie?" Sarah snapped her mouth shut. She hadn't meant to say that. Her heart sank and then rocketed into her throat with a burst of agony. How had she let that slip out?

He stared at her. Even in the low light she could see the injury she'd wielded on his face, in his eyes. *Sophie's eyes.*

"I didn't stop talking about Sophie."

Hurt and anger chased away the emotion choking off her airway. "Yes, you did. Whenever I would bring up the search—"

"I stopped," he cut her off, "talking about the search." His entire being tensed as he spoke. "I never stopped thinking about or talking about our daughter."

Sarah reminded herself to breathe and to stay calm, but that wasn't happening this side of the grave. "Our daughter was missing. Choosing not to talk about the search was the same thing. Tell the truth, Tom, you gave up on finding her."

Anger flared in his eyes. "It had been three and a half years, for Christ's sake. She was gone, Sarah. There was no bringing her back. It was time to let go and grieve. It was time to try to start living again."

"Stop. Just stop." Her body trembled with the emotions racing through her.

"You were determined to throw *us* away because we suffered the most unthinkable tragedy any parent can."

Apparently, she had tripped some sort of trigger because he wasn't letting it go.

"You didn't want us if you couldn't have Sophie, too," he accused. "You left me long before we started living apart."

"It's true." Sarah raised her chin in defiance of the emotions whirling inside her. "I couldn't go on pretending."

He said nothing.

"For the love of God," she demanded, "just admit how you really feel—how you felt then. You didn't want to talk about our daughter because you couldn't look at me and have that discussion."

He turned away then.

She shook her head. "See. You can't even talk about her and look at me now."

He whipped around and grabbed her by the shoulders. "That's not true. I stopped talking about her because I wanted you to come back to me. You left me, Sarah. When we lost our daughter I lost you, too. I was desperate to hang on, but you just kept pushing me away."

"I told you." She wasn't sure how she got the words out. His fingers were curled around her arms...his face so close she could scarcely breathe much less think. "I couldn't look at you without seeing Sophie—without seeing the truth."

"Enough," he growled. "I won't allow you to keep punishing yourself. You didn't do this, Sarah."

"Who are you protecting, Tom? Me or you? Are you that afraid your hatred for me will finally come out if you confess what you know in your heart? I let Sophie down. We lost our daughter because I made the wrong choice." Her lips trembled with the agony pulsing inside her. She had done this...

His mouth came down on hers so fast and so hard she lost her breath. His lips were hot and insistent, yet somehow soft despite the desperation in his kiss. His arms went around her, pulled her into him. She wanted to tear away...to run. She couldn't. She could only melt against him as his mouth devoured hers, making her knees weak and her heart stumble.

When he drew away just enough to draw in a harsh breath, he whispered, "I'm sorry. I shouldn't have done that."

Somehow, she managed to pull a little farther away. "You're exhausted. You need to sleep now. I'll keep watch."

"All right," he relented. "Keep your Beretta on you at all times."

"Count on it."

Sarah stood at the window and stared out into the darkness as he settled in on the sleeping bag. Her body hummed with need so powerful she could hardly hold herself still. She hadn't felt anything like this since…in more than five years. She had thought that part of her was dead.

As confused and uncertain as she felt, now wasn't the time to examine those unexpected feelings. Focus was essential. Whatever happened they both needed to be on their toes.

Minutes later when he had finally given up the fight and fallen asleep, she headed outside to check for any movement around the compound. The moon was bright tonight. The lack of cloud cover made it even colder. Didn't matter. She needed to clear her head. The way her body still shook she didn't trust herself to be in the same room with him. Incredibly, no signs of a looming panic attack had appeared. *Yet.*

The night air bit her heated cheeks as she slipped off the porch and onto the path. They had walked the path to their lookout post so many times she knew it by heart. She kept her Beretta palmed just in case. The woods were eerily quiet. She thought of Mia's grandmother's stories. Sarah didn't believe in ghosts, but she did believe in devils—the human kind. If Meltzer and his forefathers had been doing the sorts of things Mia's grandmother and Tom had suggested, there was no telling what he had planned for or perhaps had already done to the children he'd abducted.

All Sarah needed was proof they were here. She could call her chief and get the necessary paper to enter the premises.

The tinkling sound of laughter brushed her senses.

Sarah stilled, staying close to a tree for cover.

Laughter resonated through the night again. The sound was coming from beyond the iron fence. Sarah peered through the darkness. She could just make out little forms running about on the other side of the fence. Voices joined the laughter.

Definitely children, male and female. Playing.

The urge to turn on the flashlight tucked into her back pocket was nearly overwhelming.

She held perfectly still. Absolutely silent and invisible. She didn't even breathe.

Sarah eased down onto her knees to watch for a glimpse of one of the children in the moonlight. She listened intently.

Leaves rustled behind her position. Her fingers tightened on her weapon.

A hand landed on her shoulder and she knew instantly it was Tom. Relief roared through her.

He crouched next to her.

Neither he nor she risked saying a word.

The laughter reverberated through the trees, igniting adrenaline in Sarah's veins. She turned her face up to Tom's and dared to whisper, "Do you hear them?" It was the only way to be sure she wasn't delusional. She was just desperate enough to be.

"Yes."

That single world brought tears to her eyes. There were children inside that compound. Hope soared inside her.

Now all she needed was for one of them to say a name...just one name from the list of missing children waiting for her to find them.

CHAPTER TWENTY-ONE

They had changed shifts four times in the past sixteen hours. Tom had finally admitted defeat and had gotten some sleep early this morning. Sarah had crashed around noon. There had been no movement in or out of the compound today. They hadn't seen or heard anyone since hearing the children last night.

Tom wasn't sure how long he could keep Sarah playing by his rules if they didn't get a real break soon.

He moved through the trees and underbrush, working his way around the perimeter of the sanatorium property. He'd made a mistake kissing her last night. How could he have believed for even a second it was okay to do that?

Sarah didn't want him anymore. She wanted a divorce. To end their marriage, the last painful reminder of their past.

She barely tolerated being near him. To some degree, he was sure she hated him and always would.

That was the risk he'd taken when he'd admitted her to that clinic. He stalled, letting the air heave in and out of his lungs. He'd been terrified that without extreme measures he would lose her to the pain and denial.

Their daughter was gone. No force on earth was going to bring her back. Tom had accepted that reality. The agony was at times unbearable, but he had learned to live with it in the only way he knew how—to recognize his child was gone and grieve the loss whether they'd had a body to bury or not.

That decision had only made Sarah despise him more.

What the hell had Larson been thinking allowing her to be a part of the Task Force on this investigation? What had she been thinking? Tom suspected she'd needed to prove something by placing herself in such a precarious position.

Maybe he'd done the same thing, except Paul Phillips had dragged him into this nightmare. There was no backing away now. Stopping this evil was no longer just the job, it was his life's mission. He had promised Paul he would end this. It was the only way he and his family would ever truly be free of the nightmare that had devastated two generations in a small Tennessee town.

Tom wouldn't stop until it was done. What else did he have to do with his time? His career was on shaky ground. He'd lost Sarah and Sophie. The memories of his baby girl rushing to greet him at the door after work each evening filled his mind's eye. He would pick her up and swing her around, eliciting the sweetest squeals. When he hugged her, her little arms would tighten around his neck. He stopped and allowed the memories to wash over him. Stories at bedtime. Picnics in the park on Sundays. Just watching her breathe had filled him with complete happiness.

And then she was gone.

Vanished. No evidence. No ransom.

He stared at the buildings beyond the towering fence. Like the children Meltzer had taken, only for reasons Tom would likely never know.

Tom had no tangible proof, of course, that Meltzer was the one but he knew. The way Kira Gerard had spoken to him that last time Tom had recognized she was afraid of someone. He now knew Meltzer had been her superior. Cashion had named Meltzer. It had to be him.

His cell vibrated. He dug it from his pocket. A text message from Sarah.

The gate is opening.

Tom ducked deeper into the trees and broke into a run. He had to reach the tree line nearest the road before the vehicle leaving the compound moved out of eyesight.

He dodged trees, stumbled once, twice, but caught himself. By the time he reached a good vantage point, he was out of breath and too late.

"Damn it."

"I got the license plate number."

He whipped around at the sound of Sarah's voice. "It wasn't Meltzer?"

She shook her head. "Male. Mid-thirties. Nissan Maxima, Maryland license plate. I'm texting a friend who can run the plate for us."

Tom put his hand over hers. "No one can know where we are. Not yet."

She sent him one of those glares she reserved just for him and pulled her hand away from his touch. "Yeah. I got that part."

He needed water and a break. He'd made it around the entire perimeter three times. As the shopkeeper had said, there was no other way in. The cameras on the gate precluded an attempt at rushing in when a vehicle had departed as the Maxima had only moments ago. The best he could hope for was a glimpse of one or more of the children, giving Sarah reason to call her chief for a warrant.

Unless…he intercepted a vehicle headed into the facility.

"It's my turn to explore." She shoved her cell into her back pocket. "You look like you could use a break anyway."

"Yeah." He wondered if that kiss had haunted her dreams last night the way it had his. Wishful thinking. "A break would be good. I'll be back in an hour," he reminded her as he headed for the house.

"You were on patrol far longer than that," she argued.

He hesitated, didn't look back. "One hour, Sarah."

What he really needed was a cold shower to keep his mind off what he couldn't have.

Sarah watched Tom disappear into the trees. He'd been distant all day. The kiss, she imagined. It had obviously rattled him the same way it had her. He'd invaded her dreams, bringing Sophie with him. Sarah hugged herself even now, feeling cold and empty inside. From the instant her eyes had opened the warmth of his and Sophie's presence in her dreams had vanished, leaving her desolate and angry.

She wasn't angry with him about the kiss, exactly. She doubted he'd set out to kiss her. They were married for nine years before Sophie disappeared. Their relationship had once been an impossibly strong bond of love. She supposed threads of that bond, so very fragile and unraveling a little more each day, still connected them. They'd spent almost fifteen months living apart and she'd filed for divorce ten months ago. He continued to put off signing the papers. Her attorney had suggested other options, and probably at some point she would get around to choosing one.

The legalities of their relationship didn't seem important at the moment.

She walked as close to the fence as she dared, staying within the shadows and the camouflage of the trees. Guards were posted at all visible doors. There were three she could readily see. Two other uniforms patrolled the grounds. None came near the fence. No reason to, she supposed. It wasn't as if anyone was going through it or over it. The concertina wire coiled along the top would deter most even if they managed to get that far up.

Sarah paused and looked at the windows of the buildings with her binoculars. Not once in her observations had she seen anyone at the windows. Tom had sworn he'd seen a little blond-haired girl that first night. Neither he nor she had spotted anyone since. Maybe the children were only allowed to come out and play after dark. The guards were probably equipped with night vision equipment, allowing the children's activities to be monitored. The darkness prevented anyone who happened by from seeing the children, much less identifying one or all.

Too creepy.

Shivers danced over her skin as Sarah thought of those voices in the darkness last night. None of the children had used names. Were they instructed not to? Strangely, the kids had sounded as carefree as any others romping about. Had Meltzer allowed them to believe they were in a hospital or camp of some sort?

There had been no sign of him either. His car had not exited the compound. No helicopters. She supposed there could be escape tunnels.

Her phone vibrated with an incoming text. *Dr. Colton Bentley, Silver Springs, Maryland.* Since the reception out here barely allowed text messages to filter through, the ability to google was hit or miss. Getting a phone call in or out was highly unlikely. Maybe her friend wouldn't mind doing a little research on Bentley. She sent another text to her friend, Clark Helton, requesting any other available info on Bentley.

Friend. Clark Helton wasn't actually a friend. He was her DMV contact. Sarah didn't have friends. She hadn't in a very long time. All her friends as well as the other mothers she'd met during childbirth classes and for play dates had all eventually given up on her returning their calls or answering the door when they dropped by.

Sarah couldn't talk to her friends or look at them without being reminded of what she'd lost. Maybe it was selfish, but it had been her only way to survive.

Resuming her trudge through the underbrush, she focused on the investigation and what they had so far. Cashion had claimed Meltzer was experimenting with cloning. The missing children were connected by the abductor's MO and their birthplace. According to Tom, several had displayed symptoms of these random errors associated with cloning.

Meltzer was here. That had to mean his work—the children—were here. Didn't it?

The flutter of wings overhead drew her up short. She scanned the tree limbs, some already bare for the coming winter, and watched three blackbirds take flight, their distinct caws echoing in air. The birds made her think of Halloween and the stories Mia had told her about this place. Sarah was an educated woman. A well-trained police detective. Still, she wasn't immune to superstitions. Most of them were rooted in some sort of reality. What was the saying about blackbirds? They don't give up their secrets? Something like that. If Tom was right, this was about science and medicine and playing God. And plenty of secrets.

Sarah's right foot struck a rock. She pitched forward. Hit the ground hard, her lips pressed together to hold back a yelp.

Muttering curses she scrambled up onto her knees. She glanced toward the fence just to be sure no one had heard the racket and rushed over. The guards remained at their posts and the patrol was apparently on the other side of the building.

Preparing to push to her feet, she hissed another curse as she surveyed the scrapes on the heels of her hands. At least twice she had come through this same area without tripping over anything. Curious or just plain mad, she tugged at the vines and brush that covered whatever had sent her tumbling forward.

The rock was bigger than…*it wasn't a rock.*

The headstone had once stood upright, but time and the elements had caused it to deteriorate to the point that it had crumbled and it now lay on the ground. Mia had said there was an old cemetery here.

Sarah tugged at more vines and brush, her pulse hammering as she uncovered one small headstone after the other. There was a large grouping, like an old family cemetery. Trees and shrubs had grown up between them, roots uprighting some of the stones. Wild ivy and vines had intertwined with the weeds and brush completely camouflaging the stones. None had names. They were all decades old and marked by nothing other than a three-digit number. The numbers were barely legible.

A deep rumble paralyzed Sarah. Holding her breath, she dared to turn her head to the right and look toward the iron fence. A large black dog stared at her. Her heart surged into her throat. If he barked…

"Hey, boy," she whispered.

He cocked his head, those dark eyes boring into hers.

It was a Lab. Like Sam. The same color, about the same size. Labs were usually friendly. Sarah managed a smile. "You're a good, boy," she said softly. *Please don't bark.*

His tail wagged.

If she started to back up now maybe she could get well out of sight before one of the guards reached the fence.

"Caesar! Come!"

The voice was male, but far too young to be one of the guards.

Sarah burrowed into the brush. She prayed there were no hibernating snakes in here…or spiders. She was behind the tree line, but not far enough to prevent being seen if someone ventured near the fence.

A deep bark echoed around her. Not the warning kind, but the kind Sam used when he wanted to play or he thought she was playing with him. The sound resonated inside her, nudging more of those memories she wanted to keep at bay.

"Caesar, come!" the boy repeated.

Sarah's heart pounded so hard she couldn't hear herself think. The kid was very close to the fence. Another of those throaty yelps from the dog. If she could only look, the child could be one of the missing children.

"You see a rabbit, boy?"

Sarah prayed the guard wouldn't come over and start shooting into the bushes.

"We're going to be in trouble. Playing outside in the daylight is forbidden." A little girl's voice.

"I have to get Caesar," the boy argued.

"I told you that's not his name." The little girl again.

Her voice sounded so familiar—

"Step away from the fence!"

Sarah froze.

"You know better than to wander outside in the daytime."

The stern voice was likely one of the guards.

"Yes, sir. Caesar ran out the door before I could catch him."

"Go back inside *now*. Both of you," he ordered. "I will be telling the father about this."

Was this boy's father here? Meltzer didn't have children. Maybe Bentley had children here. But then the guard had said *the* father. Holding her breath, Sarah dared to part the brush enough to get a look. The boy could be one of the missing children. The reference to father only a ruse to keep the child satisfied.

When the little boy turned to tug at the dog's collar, Sarah's heart nearly stopped. *Josh.* She clenched her jaws to hold back a cry.

Not possible.

As she watched in morbid fascination another child rushed up to help the boy with the dog. This one was a girl. Maybe the one whose voice Sarah had heard. Long dark hair lay against her pink dress, a vivid contrast to the pastel color. The little girl laughed, and then glanced back at the stubborn dog.

Sarah clutched at the tree trunk. Her heart slammed mercilessly against her ribcage.

Sophie.

6:50 P.M.

"Sarah, what you're saying doesn't even make sense."

"I know what I saw."

For the first time in more than a year, Tom was terrified. Sarah stood with her arms crossed over her chest glaring at him. He'd hoped—no, no, he'd prayed that she was doing as well as she claimed. His source had insisted that Sarah came to work every day, looked good, and did a stellar job. Tom had decided she was actually doing reasonably well despite being too thin. And he was glad. But this... t*his* was worse than anything he'd anticipated.

"Think about what you're telling me," he said gently, anguish tearing at him. "You believe that little girl was Sophie."

"That's right." Her lips trembled.

His gut clenched. "And the boy was Josh Parsons."

She nodded, determination glittering in her eyes. "I'm calling Larson and then I'm going in there."

Tom grabbed her before she could get around him. "Sarah, what you're suggesting is impossible."

She glared at him. "I am not crazy, Tom."

"No one said you were crazy," he offered, his throat threatening to close. "The trouble is, you described Sophie exactly the way she was the last time you saw her."

"Except her hair was longer. It was almost to her waist." Her voice wobbled. Her eyes told him she comprehended where he was going with this and she did not want to go there. Agony flashed in her eyes.

"Sophie would be ten years old now. Josh would be eleven," he said softly.

Sarah twisted away from him. "You think I can't do simple math? I'm telling you what I saw. I can't explain it. I won't even try. Whatever you think, Tom, that was our little girl. That was our Sophie. I saw her. She wasn't more than a dozen yards away."

He reached for Sarah, she drew away from his touch. "I believe you saw a little girl who looked like Sophie." He braced his hands on his hips to prevent her seeing how they trembled. The breath he drew in was ragged with the emotions roaring through him. "I shouldn't have involved you in this."

Sarah laughed, the sound strained. "You really do think I'm crazy." She rushed up to him, grabbed him by the shirt, and shook him. "Damn you, listen to me. Our daughter is in there. Either you're going in with me to get her or I'm going alone."

He saw the defeat in her eyes as reality chased away the determination and the hope. Tears filled her brown eyes and he would have given anything to keep her from this pain. She dropped her hands to her sides.

"I'm sorry," he murmured.

"How could I have seen them so clearly?" Her lips tried to form a smile but failed, tears spilling down her cheeks. "Sam was with them." She swiped at her tears. "He growled at me, but when I spoke to him he kind of cocked his head as if he was trying to figure out if it was really me."

Tom couldn't take it anymore. He pulled her into his arms, held her close against him. "He was a good dog."

Sarah wept like a child and his own tears flowed despite his attempts to keep them in check. For five years he had wanted to take this pain from her. To find their baby and make things right again, but that hadn't happened. He'd failed her. Failed his family. Now they were just broken. Broken and lost with nothing but this case to keep them giving one damn whether they took their next breaths or not.

All this time he'd thought nothing else in this world could ever break his heart again. He'd been certain no other pain could match what he'd already suffered, but this was more than he could bear.

Sarah dropped to her knees on the floor, Tom followed. He could only repeat the same impotent words. "I'm sorry, baby. I'm so sorry."

She stared into his eyes. "Make it go away, Tom. Please, please just make the pain go away for a little while."

He held her face in his hands and slowly kissed her tears, then her trembling lips. He ran his fingers through her hair, remembering all the nights he'd dreamed of feeling that silky mane on his skin. He would have given anything to touch her like this. His fingers drifted down to the hem of her sweater and he tugged it upward. She lifted her arms, allowing him to pull it away.

For a moment, he could only stare at the sweet swell of her breasts. She reached behind her back and loosened her bra, it fell forward, and he slid it free of her arms. His breath hitched.

"You are so beautiful, Sarah."

She pulled his face down to hers. "No talking." She kissed him hard.

His sweatshirt landed on the floor next. Their jeans followed. His hands trembled as he slipped her panties down her thighs. As thin as she was, she was still the most beautiful woman he had ever seen. He wanted to relearn every inch of her. He traced the scar on her side where a bullet had snagged her all those years ago.

She pushed him onto his back and moved on top of him, guiding him into the incredible heat between her legs. The feel of her, so damned hot and tight, as she pushed down onto him had him shaking with the need to roll her to her back and drive into her over and over, but he let her do what she would. Whatever she needed, he would give.

When she had taken all of him, she tossed her head back and moaned with pleasure. Heat fired through his veins, his muscles were taut with the need to move. He wanted to touch her, to kiss her, to whisper sweet words to her…but all he could do was stare at her. She was so, so beautiful. His hands closed over her breasts as she began to rock. He watched as her movements grew more frantic and her body tensed. She cried out as release claimed her. When her movements stopped, she opened her eyes only to turn away as soon as their gazes met, but not before he saw the stark emptiness there.

When she would have moved off him, he grabbed her by the waist and rolled her onto her back. "No," he growled. "You're not using me that way. You're not using *us*."

"Get off me," she demanded. She pushed at him and he pinned her arms against the floor on either side of her head.

He kissed her when she would have protested again. He kissed her until her lips grew pliant beneath his and the resistance in her body melted away. He started to move, sliding in and out as slowly as his crumbling control would allow.

With the final waves of completion still washing over her, Sarah told herself she didn't want this. She'd wanted him to make her forget…not make love to her. She'd wanted hot, frantic sex…not this sweet tenderness.

As hard as she tried not to feel, her body rose up to meet his with each thrust of his powerful hips. His mouth set her skin on fire. His lips teased and taunted all he touched, his stubbled jaw created a delicious friction. His fingers squeezed her bottom, lifting her so he could go deeper when she was certain she couldn't take anymore. His mouth closed over her breast and suckled. She lost complete control then. Couldn't think anymore.

He touched every part of her, brought her to release again and then again, before letting go and joining her there.

For long minutes afterward, they lay together, her body nestled against his in the perfect fit that had always been theirs. He held her so tight, as if he feared she would disappear. A single tear slid down her cheek. Poor Tom. He didn't understand.

She'd already disappeared.

CHAPTER TWENTY-TWO

Coben hated this shitty place. Made him think of the prison he'd done some time in back in his twenties. His foot on the brake, he waited for the gate to swing inward.

"These are the last two, huh?" Nichols asked.

This place made his helper nervous, too. Truth was, Coben glanced at the man in the passenger seat, it should. Poor dumb bastard.

"Last two," Coben confirmed.

"I'm glad." Nichols leaned back in his seat as they rolled through the gate and it closed firmly behind them. "This job sucked." He glanced at the two sleeping kids in the back of the van. "I don't like kids."

Coben grunted. He wasn't particularly fond of kids himself, but business was business. That was why he would live to take the next job and Nichols would likely be fertilizing some plot of ground.

When they reached the garage Coben parked and hopped out. Nichols opened the sliding door and grabbed the first kid. Coben got the other one. Two girls, both five years old. Their parents were likely losing their minds about now. Too bad. People should pay better attention. Everybody was too busy these days. Too busy for the kids, leaving all kinds of openings for guys like him.

Coben ignored the white coats he met in the corridor. They kept their gazes carefully focused forward. No one looked at him or the kid in his arms. They knew it was better to pretend they didn't see.

As soon as they reached the receiving room the doc gestured to the two examining tables. Bentley was young, thirty maybe. He was Meltzer's flunky. Smart though, from all accounts. Meltzer had all sorts of hired help. Bodyguards, assassins, you name it. All anybody ever saw was the genius he was supposed to be. If all those rich folks who flocked to him only knew. He was the devil himself.

Coben wasn't afraid of the old bastard. He wasn't afraid of anyone.

Bentley carefully examined the kids and then nodded toward the envelope lying on the table next to the door.

All was acceptable.

Coben gave him a salute and turned away.

"Dr. Meltzer wants to see you in his office."

Coben turned back to the younger man. "What about?" He was done here. The sooner he was out that gate the happier he would be. Confined spaces made him antsy.

"I have no idea," Bentley said as he covered the girls with white sheets, folding them carefully at their shoulders.

"Whatever."

Coben grabbed the envelope on his way out. In the corridor, he paused. "Wait for me. I have to talk to the boss."

Nichols shrugged. "Don't be all day. I'd like to be home before dark."

Coben shot him a look that warned he should just shut up.

Meltzer's office was on the second floor. Coben considered taking the stairs, but he'd left his pills in the van. The elevator was the better option, even if the few seconds in the damned box would ramp up his tension.

The corridor was conspicuously empty as he made his way to Meltzer's office. No kids running around. No staff up here. He'd seen only two or three of the scientist types downstairs. Up here, it was totally deserted.

Meltzer's door was open so Coben went on in. "You wanted to see me."

The old man looked up. He was seventy if he was a day. Coben didn't know why the old bastard didn't retire. Greed, he supposed. Money was the drug that drove the world.

Meltzer studied him a moment. "I'm in need of your assistance, Mr. Coben."

"I thought this was the last of 'em." Hell. He was sick of hauling around kids. He had better shit to do.

"I'll be leaving tomorrow afternoon and there are a number of clean up details that need attending to." Meltzer removed his reading glasses and set them aside. "Your assistance would make what I have to do far simpler."

No way was he staying here all night. This place was too freakin' creepy. "I have other obligations. Don't you have plenty of hired muscle to take care of your business?"

Meltzer smiled. "My assets are spread a little thin just now. Would two hundred thousand take care of any inconvenience to your schedule?"

Now he had Coben's attention. "That might make rearranging my schedule worth the trouble."

"Cash," Meltzer added. "Twenty-four hours, Mr. Coben. That's all I need."

He scrubbed a hand over his face. He could do twenty-four hours. "What kind of details are we talking about?"

"I'll be dismissing my staff tonight."

Coben's gaze narrowed. "Dismissing?"

Meltzer smiled. "I think you know what I mean. I'd like you to do the same with your associate."

Coben shrugged. "No problem."

"We'll be taking care of the children as well."

Another shrug lifted Coben's shoulders. "All right." What did he care if those kids were put out of their misery? "Anything else?" He might as well know now if there were any other additional duties expected of him.

"I've taken care of the rest. You are welcome to use the guest quarters."

"Works for me."

Coben turned to go, then hesitated. He wasn't planning to mention this, but since he was staying the night maybe he should. "The scrawny guy at the gas station said his girlfriend Mia or Milly or something like that told him there was a writer or a reporter asking questions about this place."

Meltzer's demeanor shifted instantly. The news didn't sit well. "Did he get the name of this reporter?"

Coben shook his head. "Nah. Just said his girlfriend thought she was from the city. The way she talked and all. Wore high dollar running shoes."

"I want to know more, Mr. Coben. I'm sure you and your partner will be going back into town for lunch."

"Why not?"

"If you feel compelled, take care of the reporter and there will be a bonus."

"A bonus is always good."

Coben walked out of the old man's office. So Meltzer was cleaning house. He was shutting this place down and getting the hell out.

Suited Coben just fine. As long as he got his money.

And if the old bastard had any ideas about trying to off him, he'd better think again. When Coben left this hellhole of a world it would be because his ticker quit on him not because some crazy old bastard thought he was God.

CHAPTER TWENTY-THREE

Sarah twisted her hair into a braid. She couldn't remember the last time she'd braided her hair. She used to braid Sophie's all the time. Her fingers slowed in their work. How could she have believed that little girl was Sophie? Her little girl would be ten years old now.

Tom had said Meltzer had been experimenting with cloning. He believed all those missing children were clones of their dead older siblings. Could Sophie and Josh have been taken by these same people and murdered for experimental purposes? Maybe the little girl was a clone of Sophie.

Sarah dropped her arms to her sides. And maybe she really was losing her mind. Maybe this case had been the final straw.

Poor Tom. She was fairly confident the idea of her going over the edge hurt him more than it did her. Her body ached in places that had been numb for so very long. He'd made her whole body come alive with desire. He'd made her want things she knew she could never again have.

Emotion welled in her chest and she took a long deep breath to counteract it. As much as she loved Tom and she would always love him, she feared she could never be what he needed her to be. He was a good man. He deserved to live again. Once they were through this, she intended to see that he stopped waiting for her and got on with his life.

Sarah scrubbed away the damned tears. "Idiot." She was in the middle of nowhere chasing after missing children when she had no evidence they were anywhere in the vicinity and what does she do? Lieutenant Sarah Cuddahy sees her own missing daughter as well as Carla's son—only what she'd seen wasn't possible unless they'd been cloned. This was crazy.

"Dammit." She was supposed to have checked on that PI and gotten back to Carla.

Deep breath. She couldn't allow her emotions to derail what they were here to do. Whatever was going on in that compound she and Tom had to find a way in.

Sarah reached for her cell and chewed her lip. She had two text messages from Larson. He wanted to make sure she was okay. A laugh burst out of her. "Fat chance." She ignored his messages and scrolled through her contacts. Maybe the PI Mary Cashion had used could help her out. Sarah sent him a text with the details about the man Carla wanted to hire.

Her phone gave her another low battery warning. She had her charger, but there was no electricity.

Tom's car charger didn't work on her phone. Being out here without a connection for help wouldn't be smart. She needed a damned place to plug in.

She paused on a message from Clark, her DMV contact. The Maxima driver, Bentley, was a geneticist. No surprise there. She'd meant to tell Tom, but things had gone to hell.

Sarah stared at her reflection in the cracked mirror of what had once been a bathroom and couldn't deny the new glow on her face. Last night with Tom, she had to admit, hadn't exactly been hell. As wondrous and incredible as making love with him had been, there would be hell to pay going forward. It had taken her years to forget his touch. Maybe she never had. How would she find that place again where nothing except work existed?

A worry for another day. She had plenty to deal with at the moment without jumping ahead.

Last night she and Tom had agreed that if they got a visual on another child—any child—they were calling Larson. Sarah could trust Larson. Tom wasn't sure he could trust anyone right now, except her, he'd insisted. The idea that he still trusted her warmed her. It felt good in a wholly unexpected way.

She exited the ramshackle bathroom with its broken fixtures and went in search of Tom. He stared out the grimy window as he munched on a sandwich. For a moment, she watched him even if it made her heart hurt. Some part of her wanted to walk up and put her arms around him as she had a thousand times before, but she couldn't deal with touching him right now.

"I'm going into town to charge my phone."

He turned around, worry instantly lining his face.

"I thought I'd see if Mia was willing to talk some more. Since I found the headstones her grandmother told her about it's worth pursuing."

He nodded. The shadows in his eyes…*Sophie's eyes*…haunted her.

"Be careful."

"I will." She reached for her bag and the keys.

"Sarah."

She closed her eyes and rode out the wave of emotion that flooded her at the sound of his voice as he said her name.

"Whatever happens, I don't want you taking any unnecessary risks."

She straightened and searched his face. Was he planning something without her? "What do you mean?"

"If either of us is captured the other should call and then wait for backup."

The shaking started in her legs. Somehow, she managed to close the distance between them. "Don't you dare try going in there without me. You said yourself we can't tip our hand until we're sure."

"I have a feeling that white van we saw go in this morning is trouble. Meltzer is preparing for something, Sarah. I don't want those children sacrificed while we sit here waiting for the right sign to move in."

His words had her heart pumping faster. "You wait for me, Tom. You wait for me or I'll…"

He laughed, the sound painful. "You'll what? Never forgive me? Leave me?" The devastation on his face tore at her heart. "You already did that, Sarah. I have nothing else to lose."

Before her brain could catch up with her heart, she grabbed him by the shoulders and kissed him with all the hurt, uncertainty, and love, dammit, reeling inside her. When his arms crushed her against him, she wanted to weep with relief. She'd missed his strong arms so very, very much.

She drew back. "Wait for me."

"All right. I'll wait."

Sarah pulled free of his hold and left before she embarrassed herself by breaking down completely. She blinked back the tears as she headed into town. Some part of her dared to hope that if they rescued these children maybe there was a chance she and Tom could be friends. Right now, her body wanted a whole lot more. Maybe her heart did, too.

Something else to sort out later.

She parked in front of the second-hand store and climbed out. A last glance in the side mirror had her wishing her eyes weren't so red.

The bell jangled as she pushed inside. Mia looked up and smiled. "You're back."

Sarah produced an answering smile. "Like my outfit?" She opened her coat and turned around to show off her sweater and jeans.

"Love it!" Mia gestured to her cup. "Would you like some tea?"

Sarah inhaled the scent of flavored tea. "That would be great." She propped on the counter. "I've been trudging through backwoods all morning, any chance I could charge my phone while we visit?"

"Sure. Plug in right here." Mia cleared away a spot behind the counter. "I'll get your tea."

Sarah plugged in her phone and looked around the shop. Her fingers trailed over a wool scarf that caught her attention. With no competition, she imagined Mia did a healthy business here. Sarah wandered back to the counter. Dozens of photos were taped to the wall behind it. Sarah moved closer. She spotted Mia in several. Family get-togethers, she decided.

"Here you go."

Sarah looked up. "I love these old photos." She accepted the tea and savored a sip. "Oh, this is wonderful."

"Chai tea," Mia explained. "It helps me relax."

"I'll have to remember that." Sarah scanned more of the photos as she sipped her tea. She leaned closer and peered at one photo in particular. A woman, who looked very much like Mia, had her arms around a man who looked vaguely familiar to Sarah. Where had she seen him before?

The photos were from different decades. In one, she was certain the building in the background was the sanatorium. Had someone in Mia's family been hospitalized there? Was that how her grandmother had known so much?

Another photo of the man who looked vaguely familiar was tucked between two larger ones. There were five men in the photo with the woman who resembled Mia. Three men were older. Judging by their clothes, Sarah dated the photo in the late 40's or early 50's.

"Is this your grandmother?"

"Sure is." Mia tapped the man standing next to her grandmother. "That was her beau after my grandfather passed away." Mia laughed. "He showered her with gifts from his *Mother Country*."

"Where was he from?" Sarah took another soothing drink of the warm tea.

"Berlin, Germany."

Sarah swayed. The cup clattered back into its saucer. "Wow. That's…"

"Whoa there." Mia took the cup and saucer from her. "Maybe you should sit down, Sarah."

What was wrong with her? Had she forgotten to eat this morning?

The bell jangled and Sarah glanced toward the door. Her vision blurred. She squeezed her eyes shut and looked again. Two men walked into the shop. Big guys. Fortyish. Her vision blurred again.

Oh hell.

Where was her purse?

Sarah reached for the counter, but she just kept falling forward into the darkness.

3:00 P.M.

Sarah should be back by now.

Tom checked his phone again as he paced the tree line next to the road. Service was too sketchy for a call, but she could have sent a text. He'd sent her three asking where she was. No response.

Something was wrong.

The distant sound of a vehicle drew his attention to the road. Five seconds, then ten elapsed before he got a visual. The white van was coming back. He'd seen it leave before Sarah did.

When the van stopped at the gate, a second vehicle rolled up behind it.

For a moment, Tom only stared at the dark SUV that was…*his.*

He burst from the tree line, but he was too late. Both vehicles had rolled forward and the gate had closed.

Fear detonated inside him. *Sarah was in there!* Heart pounding, he pulled up the contacts on his phone and hit the number for Larson.

The call wouldn't go through. He tried three more times before giving up and resorting to text and then the screen of his cell went black.

"Damn it!"

His started to march up to that gate and demand to be let in, but he stopped himself. They had promised each other that if this happened whoever was left behind would go for help. As much as he wanted to rush after her, without backup it would be futile.

He closed his eyes and ordered himself to think. Two or so miles back there were occupied homes on this road.

Tom hit the pavement running. He pushed himself faster. He had to hurry. He couldn't bear the idea of her being tortured or…worse.

The first house came into view and Tom barreled toward it. No cars in the driveway. He didn't care. If no one came to the door he was breaking in.

He pounded hard on the door. "FBI!" he shouted in hope of setting whoever might be inside at ease.

The door opened a crack. "What do you want?"

Female. "Ma'am, I'm Special Agent Cuddahy." He showed her his creds. "I need to use your phone. There's no cell service out here."

"Go away."

Tom forced the door inward as he drew his Glock. The woman screamed. "All I need is to use your phone. Now, just sit down and I'll be out of here before you know it."

She stumbled to her chair. Somewhere down the hall a child started to cry. Hell.

"You have my word," he assured the woman more calmly, "all I want is to make a call."

She gestured to the phone.

Tom shoved his weapon back into his waistband and made the call. Larson was the only person he trusted. In Tom's opinion, the man thought of Sarah as a daughter. He would do whatever Tom asked if for no other reason than to protect Sarah.

When Larson's voice mail echoed in Tom's ear, he swore. He left a message and then considered whether he should call the local police.

Too risky.

There was one other person he could call. He made the call to Paul Phillips. He was the only person on the planet who understood just how dire the situation was.

When Paul's voice sounded in his ear, Tom chose his words carefully. "My location is Willow Creek, fifteen or so minutes outside Williamsport, PA."

"Whose number are you calling from?"

"A stranger's a mile or so from the location. He has Sarah." The words stabbed like daggers deep into his soul. "I have no backup at this time." He swallowed hard to keep the emotion out of his voice. "I'm going in after her."

Paul didn't bother trying to talk him out of going in. Instead, he took Larson's number and assured Tom he would be en route within the hour. No matter that Phillips was some five hundred miles away, Tom felt some sense of relief at having spoken to him. Paul would keep trying to contact Larson.

Tom was grateful for any backup. He just hoped it wouldn't be too late.

He placed the phone back in its cradle. "Thank you."

The woman nodded. Her little boy had climbed into her lap and was staring at Tom as if he were the boogeyman. Tom walked out, closing the door behind him. He'd have to find a way to make it up to the lady for scaring her half to death.

He jogged out to the road and broke into a run. He couldn't wait for Larson to get here. That would take hours. Hopefully, Larson could get local support.

Still, that would take time Tom didn't have.

Waiting wasn't an option. Finding a way in was the problem.

As if fate had decided to lend him a hand, Tom heard the distinct creak of the gate opening even before he rounded the bend and saw it moving.

If he ducked into the woods here he could go back to the house and wait for Larson.

The gate opened wide and no vehicle rolled through. There certainly wasn't anything on the road behind Tom.

They knew he was here. Had likely seen his text messages on Sarah's phone.

Now they were inviting him to join them.

Tom walked toward the gate, his arms up in surrender.

I'm coming, Sarah.

CHAPTER TWENTY-FOUR

503 IVY CIRCLE, ALEXANDRIA, VIRGINIA, 3:55 P.M.

Chief Reginald Larson parked in front of the senator's front steps and shut off his engine. He wasn't sure what Adams wanted to hear. Reggie had nothing except two more missing kids to report. The case was at a dead end, and he hadn't heard from Sarah in more than forty-eight hours. He wasn't sure which terrified him more, the wall they'd hit with the investigation or the idea that she was out there trying to find those kids on her own?

He could pretend she'd taken some time off as she had said, but he knew better.

His cell phone vibrated again to remind him he'd missed a call. The number wasn't one he'd recognized so he'd let it go to voicemail. Frankly, he had no desire to sit out here and return the call, keeping Adams waiting. When a senator called, a mere cop jumped. Reggie had people to answer to. The chief of police had made it clear that whatever Adams wanted or needed, Larson was to make it happen.

He got out of his car and closed the door. There was sure as hell something off about this whole situation. He trusted Sarah too much to believe Tom was as wrong as Swinwood insisted. Swinwood and the other FBI agents who'd been buzzing around Reggie's office insisted Tom was unstable. Whether he was or not, one thing was certain, he was in deep trouble.

As he climbed the steps, Reggie braced for more complaints from the senator. He had a feeling that whatever the hell was going on, the senator was eyeball deep in it. With his little girl missing, one would think he'd be all too ready to cooperate with the investigation. Instead, Adams had bucked up, done nothing but give Larson trouble, and refused to talk to Riggs. Then suddenly about half an hour ago, he called and insisted Reggie was to come see him ASAP.

He raised his hand to knock. The door was ajar. His instincts went on point as he withdrew his weapon. What the hell was going on here? He eased the door open.

The first thing he saw was Mrs. Adams hanging from a rope tied to the bannister on the second floor. Judging by the discoloration of her face she had been dead for a good while. "Mother of God," he murmured.

Reggie started forward, but stopped when he saw the senator sitting on the floor with his back against the wall. Blood had pooled on the marble

DEBRA WEBB

floor around him. His cell phone, crushed into several pieces, lay nearby.

At first, Reggie figured the senator was dead, too, then Adams turned his head and looked at him. His eyes were glassy.

Damn.

"Thank you for coming, Chief."

"Is there anyone else in the house, Senator?" Reggie turned all the way around, his weapon at the ready, scanning the entry hall and the doorways of the rooms that funneled from it.

"He's gone…"

Reggie put his weapon away and reached for his cell. "I'm calling for help."

Adams dragged in a rattling breath. "It's too late."

Reggie ignored him long enough to give dispatch his location and to order an ambulance. He shoved his phone into his pocket and knelt next to Adams. "Let's have a look."

Adams pushed his hand away. "It's too late. I'm dying. You have to listen to me."

His voice was weak and thready. He had at least two gunshots to the gut. There was a hell of a lot of blood.

"Why didn't you tell me you needed an ambulance?" Reggie felt sick to his stomach. He could have had help here by now. Hell, he'd made a stop at a drive-thru for coffee on the way. "I should try some pressure on those wounds."

Adams held up a hand, then dropped it just as quickly. "One of Meltzer's thugs came after I spoke to you." He looked up at his wife, anguish twisting his face. "He did that to her. I tried to help her before he shot me." He gasped for air. "I…didn't know he was still in the house."

"Who did this, Senator?"

"Doesn't matter. You need to listen, Chief. I'm going to tell you how to find the children."

Reggie stilled. "I don't understand." Was the man delusional?

"I want your word that you'll protect my daughter, no matter what happens." Adams made a choking sound.

"I will. I swear." If he knew where those kids were, Reggie needed him to talk fast…before it was too late. "Where are the children, Senator?"

"They're with a monster, Chief. The kind of monster you've only known in your worst nightmares."

CHAPTER TWENTY-FIVE

"Mommy?"

Sarah tried to make her eyes open, but her lids were too heavy. Warm, moist breath fanned her face just before something wet and rough slid across her cheek.

"Are you awake?"

Sarah's eyes opened. Her heart bumped into a faster rhythm. *Sophie?* A face came slowly into focus.

"Sophie?" Sarah wet her dry lips. Her throat was so dry she couldn't swallow. She was dreaming, she realized. Sophie always came to her in her dreams.

The little face smiled at her. "You've been asleep for a long time."

The big black Lab Sarah had seen at the fence, nudged her as if he wanted her to wake up now, too. Sarah tried to smile, but her lips wouldn't work right. She reached out a shaky hand, her fingers landed in the child's hair—in Sophie's hair.

Sarah smiled. "I love dreaming of you. It's the only time I can see you now."

"You're not dreaming, silly," the little girl said.

"Ah, she's awake."

Sarah jerked at the booming voice. *Male.* Her gaze sought and found the man who'd spoken.

Detlef Meltzer.

Part of her crumpled. She had been dreaming. She looked back to where the little girl had been standing expecting to confirm the precious image had been nothing but a hallucination.

But she was. The exact image of Sophie stood right there smiling at Sarah.

She jolted up into a sitting position, swayed a bit. "What is this?" she demanded of Meltzer. What had he done to her child? Was this her child? Her heart stumbled.

Meltzer smiled. "I'm quite certain you can come to the proper conclusions, Detective." He placed a hand on Sophie's shoulder.

Sarah struggled to her feet. Staggered.

"Slowly, Detective. You're still groggy from the drugs."

Drugs. The tea. Mia had drugged her…Mia knew this man. He was her grandmother's beau. The one in the photos.

Sarah reached toward the little girl. She looked from Sarah to the man whose hand rested on her shoulder.

"Go to your mother, Sophie."

A hurricane of emotions swam through Sarah as the little girl walked over and held out her hand. Trembling, Sarah closed her hand around the little girl's. She pointed a lethal glare at Meltzer. "What've you done?"

Meltzer smiled. "Sophie, take Sam to Josh. The two of you may take him outside to play while your mother and I talk."

He'd called the dog Sam…how was this possible? Were the side effects of whatever drug they had given her messing with her head?

"Can the other children go?" the little girl asked hopefully.

"Not tonight."

Sarah forced her brain to focus on the details. It was nighttime. She'd been out of commission for several hours. Where was Tom? Had he called for help?

The little girl hesitated as she reached the door. "I'll be back soon, Mommy."

"Okay, sweetie." Sarah's entire body shuddered. What had he done to her child—to…to this child?

When the door was closed and it was only the two of them, Sarah shoved aside those softer emotions. "What've you done to her? Is she…?" Sarah swallowed hard. "Is she a clone of Sophie?"

Meltzer laughed. "We have cloned many children, Detective. Most were created to give parents back the child they had lost. To clone a child is quite simple, really. For my uncles and my father the process was a major scientific milestone. For me, it was about financing my other pursuits. Like Sophie."

"So, she's not a clone?"

"She is not. She's your daughter. Just as she was when your negligence made her available to me as so many others were."

At first Sarah couldn't move. Someone had finally put blame where it belonged and the magnitude of the words spoken aloud shook her to the very core of her being. The feeling of desolation lasted only a second and then she charged up to the sick son of a bitch. "That's impossible. Five years have passed."

"Not for Sophie."

Sarah swayed again, tried to brace herself. "I don't understand." What she needed was to buy as much time as possible for her head to clear. The man didn't appear to be armed. She needed a plan. Whatever else happened, she had to escape and get these children—her child—to safety.

"I'm sure you're familiar with Cryonics."

Sarah frowned. "Are you talking about cryogenics?" She'd read a science fiction novel based on the technology years ago or maybe it was a movie. Was he insane?

"It's hardly as simple as that," he countered. "I've refined the process in hopes of preventing any significant loss of the memories and personal identity encoded in the brain. You see, the cellular damage caused by deep freezing has been the key issue all along. For decades, failure after failure has haunted science, but I have finally achieved a ninety-eight percent success rate with my two latest specimens. Sophie and Josh awoke from their Cryogenic sleep as if only a few hours had passed, not five years. Sam as well. Of course, he wasn't the first dog to be successfully brought back with little or no permanent damage."

Sarah couldn't breathe. "What you're suggesting is scientifically impossible." That much she understood.

"Until very recently that was true. It was simple enough to preserve a human in cryosleep. The trouble was in bringing them back. The result was always far too much damage on the cellular level. Irreversible damage. Many hope success will come when nanotechnology has been developed further, but I chose not to wait. The only deterrence was in having the necessary test specimens."

"Test specimens? You're talking about people—children!" Fury roared through her.

"Don't you see, Sarah? It's always been this way. In order to advance science sacrifices have to be made. None of what I have accomplished would have been possible without the children. Since picking up children on the black market often meant they had been abused or otherwise neglected, I was forced to make other choices."

"You stole my daughter." Sarah wanted to tear him apart. She wanted to watch him die screaming. Suddenly, every part of her quieted as the realization of what he was saying sank deep inside her. "You chose children for refining your technique." The words were scarcely a whisper.

The knowing smile that slid across his lips was all the answer she needed, but he wanted to brag.

"It was the perfect solution. Children's bodies are fresher, so to speak, than those of adults. Most are undamaged by the world we live in and the self-inflicted damage we do on a daily basis. Even on a cellular level their bodies are more flexible than ours. You saw the results for yourself. Sophie is perfect. She shows very little cellular damage."

Heart pounding now, Sarah steeled herself against the confusing and shattering emotions. "Does she remember her life?"

"Memories of her life are coming slowly. As soon as she saw you, she recognized you as her mother. The memories must be nudged by her senses. Whenever she is shown an image she recognizes, any memories associated with the person, place, or thing awaken. The same with the sense of smell. She recalled how much she loved cheese pizza before she tasted it. Any part of her previous life with which she comes into contact she makes the connection. This is far more than we'd dared hope for."

"You son of a bitch. You killed my little girl." Sarah lunged at him.

Two of his minions hurried into the room and grabbed her.

Meltzer straightened his expensive shirt and jacket. "I've given you a rare gift, Detective. You have your daughter back. Accept that gift with some dignity."

"Why Sophie?" Sarah had to know. "Why my baby?"

Meltzer smiled. "I saw you, your husband, and Sophie at a museum once. You won't remember, but I remember it perfectly. Sophie was so smart for such a little girl. Smart and beautiful. I knew she was the perfect candidate. I personally chose all my candidates. The work was far too important to do otherwise."

"You'll wish you were in hell before I'm finished with you, you bastard."

"I think not, Detective. You see, your husband has created quite the quandary for me and, unfortunately, I have to leave all this behind. Since I'm confident the rest of the world will be as ignorant of true science and medicine as you are, I'll be destroying the fruits of my life's work."

"No!" Sarah tried to break free. She couldn't let him harm the children…her child, Carla's child.

"Not to worry." He fastened the middle button of his jacket. "This time you and your husband will die with your daughter."

"Who did you call?"

The man's fist plowed into Tom's jaw again. He had lost count of the number of blows. He spit the blood from his mouth, his damaged lip burning like hell. "No one. There was nobody home at any of the houses and my cell was dead. I've already told you this."

The man leaned forward and put his face in Tom's. "And I still don't believe you, Special Agent Cuddahy. Now, let's try this again."

Tom braced for another blow.

The door opened with a heavy squeak and a man stuck his head inside. "Coben, the boss wants to see you."

"Coben," Tom repeated. He looked up at the bastard, his right eye swelling so fast he could hardly see out it at this point. "Nice to put a name with the face."

Coben kicked him in the gut on his way out. "Shut up."

Tom forced his muscles to relax and quieted his breathing. He needed to hear whatever he could. He had no idea how much time had passed. Six or seven hours at least. Had Larson received his message? Was Paul close? Truth was, Tom wasn't sure how much longer he could hold out.

"I'm almost finished in here." Coben said.

Tom leaned as far toward the door as possible to hear whatever was said next.

"Who he called no longer matters. Kill him. Then the woman and children."

Fear hurtled through Tom. *Sarah*. The kids. He was going to kill them all.

"I'll take care of it, Meltzer," Coben groused.

"I'm leaving in a few hours and I want to see for myself that it's done."

"Yeah, yeah," Coben snapped.

The air stalled in Tom's lungs. He had to do something. He struggled against the plastic handcuffs. Had to get loose.

Coben returned. He looked to be fifty or so. Fit. Mean as hell. The sort who killed without remorse. He rolled up one sleeve and then reached for the other.

Tom laughed suddenly.

Coben stopped rolling up his sleeve. "What the hell you laughing at?"

"For an old man, you pack a good punch."

Coben shoved the chair backwards. Tom landed on his back on the floor with a thud. The bastard's boot settled on his throat. "I might be old, but at least I'm gonna keep breathing. That's more than I can say for you, Special Agent Cuddahy."

"You're a real tough guy," Tom ground out, "with me all tied up like this. I'll bet you wouldn't be so damned tough if my hands were free."

Coben laughed. "Nichols," he shouted, "get your fat ass in here."

The man who'd stuck his head in a moment ago came into the room. He glanced from Coben to Tom and back. "What?"

Coben withdrew the weapon from his waistband and handed it to the other man. "I'm going to cut the Special Agent here loose. If, by some twist of fate, he kicks my ass, shoot him."

Nichols adjusted the weapon, the barrel aimed at Tom. "My pleasure."

While Coben jerked up the chair and stalked around behind Tom, he focused on what he had to do. He calmed his muscles. Coben's knife slide between his wrists, slitting the plastic cuffs. Tom blocked all else from his mind as he stood. Coben gave him a push.

"Let's see what you got, pretty boy."

Tom spun, slamming his right fist into the man's jaw and his left into his gut with every ounce of force he possessed.

Coben's head jerked back as he grabbed his stomach, then he grinned. "Oh, now, is that it?"

Tom thought of his little girl. A piece of crap like this had taken her. Now the lives of at least half a dozen other children were hanging in the balance. Tom tore into the man. They tumbled to the floor. Tom banged his head against the floor. Over and over. Coben tried to buck him off. Tried to get a jab in. Tom pounded his face with his fists.

"Shoot him," Coben squeaked out.

Tom rolled, pulled Coben atop him. The weapon fired. Coben's body jerked. Tom dragged him up and shoved him into the other man.

The weapon discharged again.

Tom grabbed for the weapon. He twisted it around and the next bullet entered the soft area under Nichols's chin. The man dropped to the floor.

Running footsteps echoed in the corridor.

Tom flattened against the wall next to the door.

The footsteps hurried past and eventually faded.

Sounded as if anyone who'd figured out what Meltzer was up to was attempting to escape.

Tom checked Coben's body for a radio or phone. He grabbed the cell and the fresh ammo clip in his back pocket.

Easing the door open, Tom checked the corridor.

Clear.

He had to find Sarah and the children before it was too late.

CHAPTER TWENTY-SIX

Sarah stood next to the door, her arms shaking as she held the one chair in the room high over her head. When that door opened she was taking out whoever stood in her way of her getting out. She had to find the children and…*Sophie.*

The door burst open.

Tom.

Sarah dropped the chair and ran into his arms. "Thank God you're here."

"We have to hurry."

She gasped. "Are you okay?" His face was bloody. Both eyes were swollen, one horribly so.

"I'm okay. We have to find the children before Meltzer—"

"I know." She grabbed his hand and held it tight. "Let's go."

The corridor was eerily quiet.

"I've searched this entire floor," Tom said. "The other rooms and offices are empty. Did you see anything when they brought you in?"

Sarah wished she had. "I was drugged. I woke up in the room where you found me."

Tom paused at a door at the stairwell door. Sarah held him back when he would have opened it.

"Tom."

He turned to her. It hurt her to look at his damaged face.

She steadied her voice. "Sophie and Josh are alive. It was them I saw. Sam, too." The tears wouldn't be contained, hard as she tried.

"How is that possible?"

"When we're out of here, I'll tell you everything Meltzer told me."

"You saw him?"

She nodded. "He's here."

"Not for long." Tom reached for the door. "I didn't have a visual, but I heard him tell his goons to kill us and the children. He said he was leaving. We have to stop him. If he gets away…"

He didn't have to say the rest. Sarah understood. He would just set up shop someplace new. The idea of him doing what he had done to Sophie and the others to more children was unfathomable.

In the stairwell Tom headed up rather than down. They all but ran up the stairs. The third floor corridor was as deserted as the one on the second floor had been. The rooms were offices and most were deserted. Computers still on…Coats and briefcases still at desks.

A body was slumped over the desk in the fourth office they entered.

"Is he alive?" Sarah didn't see any blood.

Tom checked his pulse then shook his head.

They moved on to the next office. Again, the man behind the desk was dead, this one leaned back in his chair. A foamy froth had bubbled from his lips.

Sarah pointed to the coffee cup. There had been coffee at the other man's desk. "They've been poisoned."

"Don't touch anything," Tom warned. "Let's keep moving."

They found the same in the remaining offices. The rooms were either empty or the person occupying that office was dead. As they reached the stairwell door once more, Tom hesitated. He surveyed the corridor they had just searched.

"They'll start a fire to destroy all of this…or blow it up. They left too much evidence, Sarah. The computers and file cabinets. We have to move faster. Hopefully we'll find the children on a lower level."

"If we're not too late." Sarah's heart ached.

They rushed down the stairs. Other than a few more dead staff members, the second floor was deserted. Doors standing open. Fear pounded in her veins. They found the same on the first floor, leaving only one more level—the one below ground. There was a chance Meltzer's goons had herded the children there, making it more difficult for them to escape.

The basement was deathly quiet. Tom moved with caution, Sarah right behind him. There were no offices in the basement. The rooms were labs. This was where Meltzer had executed his experiments on God only knew how many children. The labs as well as the equipment were cutting edge. She wasn't a scientist, but she recognized the advanced technology.

In one of the rooms, bodies were suspended in large freezer like storage containers. Sarah didn't recognize the faces behind the windows in the containers. The bodies were adults—elderly adults. She hesitated at the final container. The woman inside was Mia's grandmother.

Sarah understood now. This was where he kept those in cryosleep.

Had Sophie been here all this time?

"We have bodies."

She hurried back into the corridor to find Tom. He stood at the doorway to another of the labs. She joined him there. The guards they had watched patrolling the compound had been called to this room and executed. All had gunshots to the backs of their heads.

Fear tightened its grip on her chest. "We're running out of options. Where are the children?"

There was only one more door. On the left, a few yards ahead.

They reached the door. It was locked. Tom peered through the small window in the upper part of the door.

"They're in there." He turned to Sarah. "A dozen or more kids."

Sarah's attention had stalled on the electronic keypad on the wall next to the door. Her eyes read the words, but it took a moment for her brain to assimilate the meaning.

Warning…extermination will begin in 90 seconds… 89…88…

"We have to get them out." Fear twisted inside her. "We have to get them out now! They're supposed to die in there."

"Stand back." Tom leveled his weapon, taking aim at the keypad.

Sarah grabbed his arm. "The children?"

"They're huddled together in the far corner."

"But, what if—?"

"It's a risk we have to take."

He was right. They had no other choice.

Tom fired four shots, two at the keypad and two at the door handle. He tried the door. It still wouldn't budge.

50 seconds…49…

Sarah watched, defeat tugging at her, as Tom fired two more shots around the handle. An alarm sounded and the screen on the keypad turned red and started to flash.

Airlock has been compromised. Extermination has been cancelled.

Sarah cried out with the relief flooding through her. Tom slammed his weight against the door. She checked the corridor, just in case the alarms brought any backup Meltzer might have on hand—unless he'd killed them all.

The door gave way and Tom lurched into the room. Sarah was right on his heels. The children stared at them in fear. For a moment Sarah and Tom couldn't move. They could only stand there staring at all those little faces.

The group of children parted and Sam trotted over to them, his tail wagging.

"Mommy! Daddy!" Sophie ran to them next.

Tom dropped to his knees.

Sarah tried to catch her breath, tried to staunch the tears. Impossible. The sound of sobs pulled her attention away from the tender scene. The other children were crying. They were afraid. They wanted their families, too.

"It's okay now, boys and girls." Sarah motioned for the children to follow her. "We're taking you home."

Tom carried Sophie and Sarah urged the rest of the children forward. They headed for the stairwell. Sam trotted ahead as if scouting for trouble. God, how she loved that dog.

They reached the first floor without incident. Sarah ushered the last child through the stairwell door. Tom handed Sophie to her. The weight of her child in her arms had love and happiness bursting in Sarah's chest.

"I'll have a look outside first. Don't bring the children out until I give the word."

Sarah nodded, unable to speak.

Tom eased open the door on the west side of the building and scanned the perimeter. This was the side of the building he and Sarah had been watching from the tree line. No guards. No vehicles.

He moved back to where Sarah and the children waited. "Lead the kids over to the far corner of the property near the fence where we hid in the tree line." He handed her the phone he'd taken from Coben. "Keep trying to get through to help just in case Larson didn't get my message."

Sarah accepted the phone. Worry showed in her eyes. "What're you going to do?"

"If Meltzer is still in the compound I'm going to find him. Now go."

Tom watched until Sarah and the children were nearly to the fence, then he rushed toward the opposite side of the building. When he'd entered the gate, he'd noted the driveway continued on toward the other side of the building. There had to be a parking area between the buildings. If Meltzer was still here he would likely be loading up to get the hell out.

When Tom reached the corner on the east side of the building his suspicions were confirmed. A parking garage stood about twenty yards from the main building. On top was a helipad with a waiting helicopter.

Tom scanned the open area between him and the garage. Clear. He moved out and headed for the garage. As he reached the entrance an explosion sounded behind him. He dove for cover. Three more explosions rocked the ground. The next sound was the building he'd just exited falling in on itself.

Raised voices drew his attention upward.

The garage roof.

Tom scrambled up and moved into the garage. He searched for the nearest stairwell. The whirr of the helicopter's engine starting had adrenaline roaring through him. He could not let that bastard escape.

He spotted the stairs and started upward. At the roof landing Tom cautiously opened the door and had a look. Meltzer and a man wearing a white lab coat were arguing. Tom couldn't hear them over the chop-chop of the helicopter blades, but the body language left no question that the man in the white lab coat was not happy.

Another blast rent the air and both men turned to stare toward the south.

Tom couldn't see what the blast had taken out, but his guess was the gate. He hoped that meant backup had arrived.

A weapon discharging drew his attention back to the men. The man in the white lab coat was down. Shoulders hunched around his head, Meltzer hurried toward the waiting helicopter.

Tom rushed after him. "Stop right there, Meltzer!"

Meltzer kept going. Tom fired at the rooftop a few feet in front of him. Meltzer didn't slow. Tom resisted the urge to put a bullet in his brain and went after him. They needed this bastard alive to help the children. God only knew what he'd done to them and the only files may have just been destroyed.

Just before Meltzer would have climbed into the helicopter, Tom threw himself against the older man. They went down together. As they rolled and struggled, Tom fought to keep the barrel of Meltzer's gun away from him.

The helicopter lifted off.

Meltzer's attention shifted to his departing escape route. He screamed at the pilot, his voice lost to the cacophony of sounds.

Tom ripped the weapon from his hand and tossed it aside. "It's over, Meltzer."

Meltzer's cold, hard gaze zeroed in on Tom and he started to laugh hysterically.

Tom got up and yanked him to his feet. "This is the end, Meltzer."

"No, no, you're wrong. It's only the beginning. Now the world will finally know my genius," Meltzer announced. "No more hiding. I'll be in all the history and science books. Right where my family has always belonged."

"Whatever." Tom guided him toward the stairwell door. "As long as you're behind bars where *you* belong."

When he and his prisoner exited the garage, official vehicles, ambulances, and cops were all over the place.

"It's about time," Tom said to Larson.

"I got here as fast as I could," Larson said as he took custody of Meltzer. "I brought the cavalry with me."

"I can't tell you how much I appreciate that," Tom admitted.

Paul Phillips cut through the crowd of cops and agents. He reached for Tom's hand and pumped it hard. "You did it, old friend. You finished it. I can't thank you enough."

Tom gave him a nod. "It's good to see you, man."

Paul grinned. "I owed you a rescue."

"Tom!"

He turned and watched as Sarah and Sophie hurried toward him. Sam was right on their heels.

Tom dropped to his knees and hugged his family.

WILLIAMSPORT REGIONAL MEDICAL CENTER, OCTOBER 27, 6:00 A.M.

Tom's face was looking better after a half dozen or so ice packs. His knuckles were scraped and his shirt was a little bloody, but otherwise he looked so damned good to Sarah. They were all alive and that was what mattered.

Her head had finally cleared of the drug hangover. She'd wanted to stay with Sophie and Josh while the doctors examined them, but Larson and Phillips had insisted she and Tom have coffee and food. She was glad now that she had agreed. She felt human again.

Soon the exhausted and relieved parents of the children they had rescued would be filtering in. Except for Katie Adams and Cassie Cashion's parents. Katie's aunt, her mother's sister, was en route from Richmond. She and her husband would take care of Katie. Cassie's grandmother was coming for her. Chief Larson had kindly ordered a police escort for Carla Parsons. She, too, would be here any minute. The FBI was all over the compound. Thankfully, Meltzer's briefcase had contained electronic copies of his files. He would never have simply blown up his life's work. He wanted the world to know.

Paul Phillips gave Sarah a hug. "I should get back on the road."

"Thank you," Sarah blurted before she lost her nerve. "For today and…for before. You tried to help when Sophie first went missing and I never thanked you. It means a lot that you came."

Phillips nodded. "I was in a bad place then."

Sarah smiled. "You're good now though and that's what counts."

Phillips looked healthy and vibrant. He'd showed Sarah and Tom photos of his family. It was obvious the man was immensely happy. He gave her a nod before saying goodbye to Tom. The two had helped each other survive their worst nightmares.

Speaking of good friends, Sarah turned to the man who was also her boss. "Thank you, Chief, for believing in us when no one else did."

He hugged Sarah hard. She felt his tears against her forehead. In reality, Reginald Larson had been like a father to her. He'd been there when she thought nothing would ever be right in her world again. She was so grateful she could share this incredible moment with him. All this time she'd thought she no longer had any friends and she'd been wrong.

"I expect you back to work," he warned. "I know you and Tom will need some time off but I don't want to lose my best detective."

"Not going to happen, Chief."

When Phillips was gone and the chief had hurried off to greet more arriving parents, Sarah sat down in the small waiting room. She was exhausted, but in a good way. She couldn't wait to take her baby home.

Tom sat down next to her. "I guess we did pretty good."

She laughed and almost started cried before she could get what could only be called a moment of hysteria under control. "We did damned good, Agent Cuddahy. " The FBI director himself had shown up at the hospital to check on the children and to thank Tom. Sarah suspected he'd be getting a promotion soon and Swinwood would be closing his investigation.

Tom took her hand in his. "I want us to be a family again, Sarah." When she would have interrupted, he held up a hand for her to wait. "I know it won't be easy. We have things to work out. But I want to try."

Sarah leaned toward him, grimaced at his bruised and battered face. "I can promise you one thing, Tom Cuddahy. There is no force on earth that will be able to tear us apart again. We are a family. We fell apart for a while, but that's not happening again." She gently brushed her lips across his. "You're stuck with me."

He pulled her against his chest. "I love you, Sarah. I've never stopped loving you."

She put her hand over his heart, so very thankful for the rhythmic beating there. They could have both been killed. "I know. And I never stopped loving you, no matter how much I denied it." She intended to get the counseling and whatever else she needed and to stick with it for as long as it took this time.

The door opened and a nurse motioned for them. "You can see Sophie now."

As they followed the nurse to Sophie's room, Sarah held onto Tom. As happy as this moment was, there were still dark moments to come. "I suppose there will be extra tests and follow up exams for Sophie and Josh."

"That's a safe bet."

"I just don't want any of these children turned into guinea pigs." They'd been through enough already.

"I've been assured the children will be protected. We can only hope the powers-that-be will stand by their word."

Maybe Paul Phillips had the right idea. He'd taken his family and disappeared.

The nurse paused at a door. "Go right on in."

Tom thanked her. Before they went into the room to be with Sophie, he lifted Sarah's chin and looked deep into her eyes. "I will protect you and Sophie. You don't need to worry about that."

She smiled. "I know."

Tom opened the door. Sophie sat on the exam table with her little legs swinging and Sam was sprawled on the floor beneath her feet. The hospital had allowed him to stay with her under the circumstances.

"Mommy! Daddy!" Sophie beamed a smile. "The nurse gave me a lollipop." She waved the cherry red treat.

Sarah hopped up on the table next to her. "Red lollipops are your favorite."

"I know that now." She licked the candy. "I had to try a blue one and a yellow one before I remembered it was the red I liked best."

Sarah and Tom exchanged a glance. Meltzer had said that would be the case. On some level Sarah was grateful he was alive just in case problems cropped up that only he could answer. Still, she hated what he had done and wanted to see him pay.

"Can we go home now?" Sophie looked to her dad. "I'd like to sleep in my bed tonight."

Sarah smoothed a hand over her daughter's hair. "I hope so. We'll have to see what the doctor says."

A light rap sounded at the door before it opened. Chief Larson stuck his head in the room. "Sarah, do you have a moment."

"Sure." Sarah hopped off the bed. "I'll be right back." She left a kiss on Sophie's forehead.

When she was in the corridor and the door to Sophie's room closed, she searched her boss's face for any indication there was new trouble. "What's up?"

"Carla Parsons is here and she wanted to see you for a moment."

Sarah's heart lifted. "Of course."

"She's with Josh just a few doors away."

Larson showed Sarah to Josh's room. Sarah knocked on the door.

"Come on in," Carla called.

Inside Josh and his mom sat side by side on the exam table. Carla instantly hopped off the table and rushed to hug Sarah.

"Thank you." Tears glittered in her eyes. "I don't have to tell you what this means."

Sarah hugged her again. "We found our babies."

"I am forever in your debt," Carla said, her words broken.

"No." Sarah took Carla's hands in hers and squeezed. "*You* are the one who never gave up. I am in your debt."

Carla nodded, too emotional to speak.

"Call me if you ever need anything," Sarah insisted before waving goodbye.

She hurried back to Sophie's room and cracked the door open just enough to watch her little girl and her daddy together.

Before…Sarah had loved standing at Sophie's bedroom door at night watching Tom read bedtime stories to her. Sarah had been certain she would never again be able to share a precious moment like that with her family.

Those fears were behind her now. She had her family back and at least one monster who stole children for his own evil purposes had been stopped.

Sarah joined Tom and Sophie. Sam sat his head on the exam table, wanting some of the attention and they all laughed.

The nightmare was over.

Have you read BONE DEEP? Order it now!

A NOTE FROM THE AUTHOR

Thousands of children are reported missing each year. Of those, a hundred or more will be murdered. Please pay attention to the children around you. If something appears wrong, or simply a little off where a child is concerned, please make the effort to determine if the child is safe. Don't be afraid to speak up. Never allow a child to be harmed on your watch. Contact your local Department of Human Services or just call 911.

ABOUT THE AUTHOR

Debra Webb, born in Alabama, wrote her first story at age nine and her first romance at thirteen. It wasn't until she spent three years working for the military behind the Iron Curtain—and a five-year stint with NASA—that she realized her true calling. A collision course between suspense and romance was set. Since then she has penned more than 100 novels including her internationally bestselling Colby Agency series. OBSESSION, the first novel in her romantic thriller series the Faces of Evil, pro-pelled Debra to the top of the bestselling charts for an unparalleled twenty-four weeks and garnered critical acclaim from critics and readers alike. Don't miss a single installment of this fascinating and chill-ing ten-book series!

Visit Debra at www.thefacesofevil.com or at www.debrawebb.com. You can write to Debra at PO Box 10047, Huntsville, AL, 35801.

Made in the USA
Middletown, DE
28 October 2014